THE LOST TWIN

BOOK II

OUIDA D.W.

info@barringerpublishing.com

Barringer Publishing, Naples, Florida
www.barringerpublishing.com

Cover Art by Sara Tarr
Interior Sketch Illustrations by Frances O. O'Neal

ISBN: 978-1-954396-66-1
Library of Congress Cataloging-in-Publication Data
Gilda: The Lost Twin / Ouida D.W.

Printed in U.S.A.

Dedication

For every reader who finds this book, may you find truth, healing, and life in these words.

To the written word and to art, the most cathartic and impactful form of expression.

And to the Kingdom, may God do what he will in every soul who reads this book.

OUIDA D. W.

Table of Contents

PROLOGUE

GILDA

PAST
7 YEARS OLD

Island of Ozmandia

I had lost my way. The sun was deep scarlet and melting behind the line of cypress trees.

"Sunbeam? Whitewing? Anyone out there?"

Silence.

Hours had passed. So, I decided to head home.

It was the first time Sunbeam had never found me. That day, I ventured farther into the forest than ever before. I knew the other kids wouldn't search that deep in the brambles—they'd be too scared. And the terrifying truth felt like a punch in my belly; no one would be coming to my rescue.

I was alone. The darkness crept in as the last slice of orange sun dropped behind the skyline.

Let's see . . . let's see . . . is that the path? No . . . no . . . My thoughts raced. *We always played hide and seek—this never happened. Usually, Whitewing could sense my trail. Where were they?*

Another hour had come and gone. Then another . . . and another . . .

"Hello? Anyone out there?"

Silence.

By that time, it was pitch black. OWOOOO! A wolf howled, which startled me because it sounded close—too close. And I became too terrified to keep walking. I stopped to catch my breath and hid behind some foliage. I glanced up. Horrified, the large tree branches blew in the wind and looked like giant ogres raising their arms over me. My heart started to pound. I realized I wasn't just lost; I was *very* lost.

This was the first time I'd ever been alone in the dark without knowing my way. Even as a small child, I knew the forest well, but this time, I went too far!

"Father? Mother?" I cried. "Sunbeam? Whitewing?"

Terrified, I shut my eyes, too afraid to see what the large ogre trees might do next. "Oh please. God, help me." I whispered.

Suddenly, there came a soft breeze that rustled the leaves. But it was a new kind of breeze that felt cool and refreshing on my face. Then it felt as if someone touched my back. And I opened my eyes, and before me—I saw a man. His face glowed radiantly, and he looked very kind.

"Who . . . who are you?" I muttered in disbelief. His eyes were golden brown and sparkly.

"Little one, you have left the path to walk in darkness," he said. "Do not worry. I will guide your feet toward the right way." He sat down next to me and smiled. It was the kindest smile in the world.

"Where did you come from?" I asked. "And why are you so bright?"

"Child, when you walk in the night, and stumble, I am your light."

"Can you help me? How do I find my way back?" I cried.

He reached down and wiped my tears. "Little one, do not be sad." Then he gave me a little seed. "Take this seed. Keep it with you. It sprouts in darkness but blooms in the sun. The sun will always rise." Then he put his hands over my eyes, and when he lifted them, I saw a streak of white moving across the forest. It was Whitewing, my horse! He was galloping in the far distance. "Oh, thank you, sir! Thank you!" I turned to hug him, but just as quickly as he came, he was gone.

"Whitewing! Whitewing! I'm here! Over here!"

In the next second, Whitewing sped toward me. Sunbeam was riding on his back.

"Gilda!" panted Sunbeam. She jumped off Whitewing's saddle and squeezed me. "We were worried sick! It's pitch dark out here. We barely heard you screaming for us. How did you see us that far away?"

"A man . . . he showed me."

"A what?" The whites of her eyes darted back and forth. "What man? Gilda, there's no one out here in the dark but you."

"But I saw him. He was here! He talked to me! He gave me this seed!" I opened my hand to show her the seed.

"OK, Gilda, whatever you say," she smirked. "Looks like this has you all worked up. Let's get back before Mother starts to worry."

We jumped on Whitewing's back. Sunbeam took the reins while I held onto her waist. My fear faded as we sped out of the dark canopy of ogres. And I turned back to see if I could spot the man that glowed like light.

"Where are you?" I muttered under my breath.

And although I didn't see him, I heard his voice in the breeze, over the sound of Whitewing's pounding hooves: *Child, when in darkness, know the sun will come soon.*

Come soon? What does that mean?

"Sunbeam, did you hear that?"

"Hear what, Gilda? You've been in the dark too long. Time to get you home!" And she snapped the reins, sending Whitewing into a full gallop. I squeezed the seed tightly in my hand.

Over the years, as I grew, I stopped looking for him. And because I stopped looking, I assume I stopped seeing. Sometimes he'd cross my mind, and I wondered if he was still out there. But one thing is for sure, I never forgot him. Because I had squeezed that seed so tightly, it left a scar in the palm of my hand.

GILDA: THE LOST TWIN

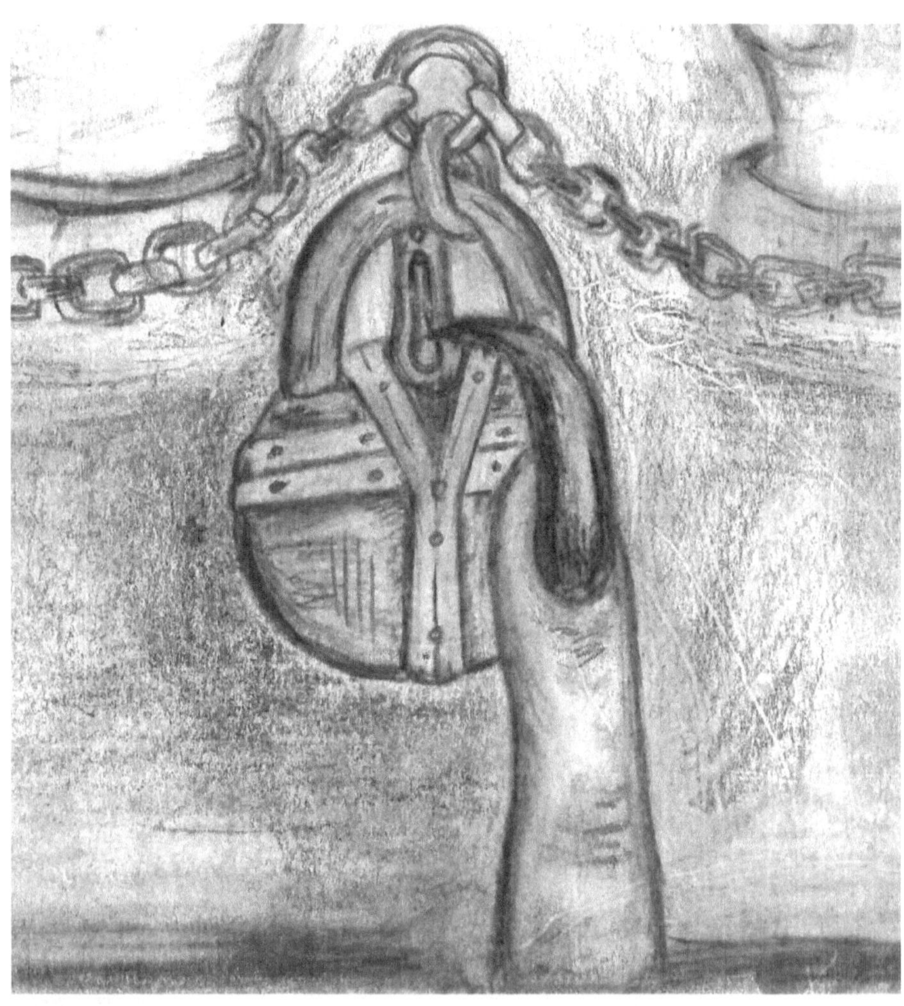

THE BEGINNING OF THE END

GILDA

PAST
13 YEARS OLD

Valley of Dry Bones

"She has come. She is here in the Valley," said Lord Wolford. His icy blue eyes gleamed with sinister intent. He shook his head in disbelief and paced back and forth.

And there I lay, beaten over and over again with his questions. "What is your decision?" he asked.

My heart felt hot and skin blue under the pressure of his lashing, and I winced with every breath I inhaled. "Do what you must," I muttered. I presumed the outcome would be torturous yet made up my mind. I wanted to escape. I knew what I had to do.

"She has come to see you. Why would you . . . for someone who cares so little?" mocked Wolford. "You've lain here years while Sunbeam runs free."

"I cannot undo what's been done," I said. It hurt to release those words from my lips. I wanted justice, but not the way *he* wanted it. In the instant I felt the betrayal poison my bones, I should have closed the door on Sunbeam forever. But I did not. I could not. Why? This door would stay open until I was avenged, not his way, but *my* way.

I remember the night all too well: a haunting dream that permeated every second of my reality. The night he stole me from my bed five torturous years ago.

"What is your answer?" asked Wolford.

"I . . . I . . ." I couldn't answer him. At this point, I was on the edge of death and wondering how much more I could take.

He slammed his claw down on the table. "She has come. Your time here is up unless you bring Sunbeam to me. She is powerful, not easy to defeat. But you, Gilda, are the leverage I have to win this battle."

"I . . . I . . ." my mouth felt sealed behind a heart that wasn't broken anymore but numbed after too many heavy circumstances.

He raised his claw into the air, ready to plunge it into my chest. It was urgent. In one instant I could be dead, or in the other instant—free.

"I . . . I . . ." my decision would change everything.

❧ ❧

In the next second, my contemplation broke with Sunbeam's screams and the beating of Whitewing's running hooves, which aligned with the pounding of my heart. I had to make my choice. Hidden and chained behind the stone aperture, my beloved Sunbeam could not hear nor see me, but I heard her, and her words struck my heart like blades of thunder.

"Gilda? Gilda! Where are you? Where are you? Gilda!" She shouted over and over.

Why had she finally come? Was this another game? Could I trust her? The only thing I did know was we were bound together: Twins. My freedom depended on hers, and hers, mine. Mutually doomed—but only one would go free.

Her demands continued as she searched and searched for me while I lay bound behind the thin division of the chamber.

"Where is Gilda? Tell me where she is!" Sunbeam kept shouting to Wolford's minions, those bony golgums. I wanted nothing more than to shout back to my twin sister from under the chains, but I remained silent, knowing my decision would either be fatal for her, or for me. So, I lay in the silent suffering that had shackled me every day and night for years—since the night he stole me from my bed.

"Sweet Gilda," hissed Wolford. "Sometimes victory is sweet, sweet sorrow. Sunbeam is out there slaying half of my kingdom! You have the power to lure her. Then your beloved, your betrayer, will be mine, and you can go free. You or her. My offer has not changed." His blue eyes glazed over with a cold, blank stare, and he lifted his chin, sniffing toward Sunbeam's direction like a hungry lion. Swiftly, he sharpened his claw.

It was urgent. I had less than seconds to make my choice. The best I could do was the right thing—but what if that thing were wrong?—but the worst thing I could do was nothing at all.

Little did he know, the mantra in my head was that I would get revenge *my* way on her, not his.

In the next moment, the devil dropped and crawled quickly toward me—a savage animal. I looked up to find his smooth neck inches from my face. He reached behind me. The beating of his pulse was steady on the skin of his throat. "Be still," he whispered, "your freedom is near." He subtly growled and ran his claw down my back until it reached the point of the lock-shank, then further until the point of his claw stopped at the aperture of it. "Say the word," he said. His breath was warm against my face; his body felt heavy as he leaned on top of mine, smothering me. "The clock has struck, and Sunbeam has come. Say the word. I hold the key to the lock. What is your answer?"

"I'll say it . . . I . . . I . . ." In an instant, adrenaline rushed down my body. I could barely breathe. In the next second, the gods must have given me the opportunity I needed to make my choice because I felt the crossguard of his dagger at my fingertips. I knew I could take him, end it right there. Within seconds, I summoned my powers: "In the name of justice, and for revenge," I murmured under my breath. In a flash, I ejected the sharp tip of my wing like a switchblade from beneath my skin. I raised my forearm. Before he knew what happened, his cheek was streaming a river of blood from the blow I delivered to his face. He whirled woozily.

Swiftly, I drew the blade from his sheath and held it at the back of his neck. "No. You are a liar—YOUR doom is near," I whispered. "In the unlocking of my chains, you will be locked up forever. Now, release me."

Cautiously, and still woozy, he stuck the point of his claw in the aperture. The lock released with a loud snap, echoing through the chamber. I stood up. I kept the blade steady on his neck.

Sunbeam, still searching for me, must have heard the clamor because on the other side of the chamber she yelled, "Who's there? Show yourself!"

"Sunbea—" I began to disclose and shout my location until Wolford interrupted.

"Be careful," he panted, breathing through his bloody pain. "Is this the end of your pitiful story? If Sunbeam escapes this valley, one order from me, and before you can think, you are over. Every golgum in this valley will rush upon you in seconds. You *will* die in this valley! You know what to do, little wolf."

In that same moment, the bony golgums were outside the chamber. I could hear them as they began swinging their blades toward Sunbeam. Clanging swords, hooves, and insults echoed through the chamber into one maddening sound. I had less than seconds to decide: to remain in forever silence—or—free my life and end hers.

"Beloved Gilda, not everything should be said," smirked Wolford. He traced the shape of a heart over my chest with his claw. "Serve me, and at the taking of your unfaithful twin's soul, you will live."

The sounds of the clanging grew louder. "You want to do the moral thing?" mocked Wolford. "Justice is your duty. Only wolves defeat wolves. Choose yourself. You have the right to live!"

"Yes, but not on your terms," I said. "This is my story to avenge."

In some sense, he was right. I didn't deserve the last five years. And yes, it *was* Sunbeam's fault. Although the chains I wore every day were heavy, the poison of her actions and my resentment made my bones ache all the more. Over and over, my mind replayed five hard years. And now, Sunbeam had come to make it all right. But it was too late. Besides, after all she'd done, could I trust her?

Like waves, the risk of the wrong decision swept over me in heavy blows and breakers, intermixed with fears that kept me frozen, but to not act at all was more terrifying than ever.

Forced to do the *hard* thing, the only way out was . . . to kill my *beloved.*

CHAPTER ONE

GIL'DA

PRESENT
13 YEARS OLD

Holding cell, Realm of the Dark Night

Where am I? What happened? Wait. I'm here now? What day is it?

That's right. I'm no longer in Wolford's dungeon, but for the last nine months now, I'm still peering back into that hellhole. And how I got locked in this cell with nothing but a mysterious doorman that brings food and water? I don't know. But I sense it's connected. Surely, Wolford hadn't cut my silver cord, or, did he? No sorceress wants her silver cord cut; then you're lost in the astral plane, forever floating in a celestial abyss, unable to return to body. I slap my cheek to make sure I'm in my own skin.

The last thing I remember is that devil hissing, "You or her. If you fail to bring Sunbeam to me, this will be your end." Then—POOF! I wake up in this strange, dark cell. I don't know where I am. I only know time is running out. These walls are closing in. I have to get free.

My eyes feel heavy as two rocks as I fight to open them. A dim ray of green light glints through the slits of my half-open eyelids. *Where's this green light coming from?* My vision is hazy. I reach for my elixir, but it's still not there. *Wait—where is it?*

Did I take all of it? I reach further, but my hands swipe air. Nothing. *The doorman took it from me!*

Ahh! What the . . .

The more I wake, I try to rouse my limbs, but they don't budge. I'm frozen in that place between dreams and consciousness. I lie on a cold, cell floor with only a straw mat for a bed. The concrete feels like blades of ice against my bare skin.

I turn my sore neck and look down—a shooting pain—I flinch—something freezing like fire burns my hand. My eyes discover a mysterious, small object. Strangely, it's the same thing responsible for this annoying, spooky green light in my black cell. It just lies there and subtly glints on the floor near my mat. In the next moment, a haunting presence sends a chill down my neck.

"Who's there?"

My eyes come clearer into focus. I attempt to get a closer look at it. *What the . . . ? Should I even attempt to touch this thing?* If I only had my *Book of Shadows*, the magical, ancient grimoire of all grimoires, I'm sure it would have the answer. But I don't have it. Not anymore.

Cautiously, my fingers run over this mystery, dabbing its cold, hard texture. It's a . . . a . . . stone? A green crystal! Now, I know stones well, have both studied them and manipulated them for my magic. But how on earth did this one get in here? I lean forward to get a closer look and pick it up. Its texture is smooth and slippery, like that of a snake. Strangely, now in the palm of my hand, it sends an icy surge up my arm and into my chest. It seems to bite like a serpent.

The crystal glitters like magic in my hand, a bedazzling piece of jewelry that beckons me to wear it. In the next moment, it casts a serpentine prism. It shimmers spooky, green shadows against the walls as if inviting me to stare more closely, like it has something it wants me to see. But whatever it is, I sense it's too horrendous to face. I throw down the stone.

I want my elixir, nothing more than to fall back into numbed sleep. It's my time to rest. To be alone. Besides, with all the chaos I've had, I could, after all, just be *imagining* things.

Whatever this mysterious crystal wants, I am declining. There had been enough horror the last five years of my life. I was done. The past was over. And it was there I left it. No thanks!

In the next moment, this strange stone, as if knowing I'm refusing it, starts clanging on the cell floor, arresting my attention. It casts deeper hues of green light on the iron wall. Slimy and eerie, it swells greener and greener.

Then, before I even have time to think, a chilling wind picks up and begins to howl through the bars of my cell. My pulse quickens. The wind gusts harder. It blows and blows until I'm surrounded in a whirlwind. And I'm growing sick in the chilling agony of it. Then the wind starts to howl and moan like angry phantoms awakening from a graveyard.

"Go! Go away from me!" I scream, shuddering in horror.

And what starts up next, I can't bear. I clutch my ears—because in the tempest of that ghoulish wind—coming through every bar and crack of my cell, cry all the voices from the past—like ghosts—as if all the people I left behind were now surely waking from the dead to come back and haunt me.

And even more terrifying, the green crystal starts to burst and sputter green flecks that slither like snakes in the air. I can't turn away no matter how hard I try. The cryptic crystal seizes my eyes. The prism of the stone captivates my entire being as though in a trance. Then frightfully, the shadows morph.

The voices grow louder—louder! "Ahhh! Doorman!" I scream, but the voices dismiss my pleas and begin to materialize into faces. Their faces—the ones I'd left behind! *No! It's over! They're over! It's all over. I'm just imagining things!*

"Doorman! My elixir! Elixir!" At this point, I'm shaking all over and swooning.

Nervous, awfully nervous, my heart feels frozen in terror and goes completely cold. And what comes next chills me to the bone: glaring back at me through the hologram cast by the stone—something bounds into view—and all the faces meld into *one* large face that looms over me. I stare transfixed—until I recognize it as . . . as . . . my very own face! Staring back at me in horror. But not as my thirteen-year-old self now, but eight-year-old me back then. Eight years old: the time in my life when this whole horrible narrative began.

Then what comes next silences me entirely, like when you're too stunned to speak or think, and can do nothing but hold your breath and wait for what's about to happen. In the next moment, the crystal vibrates. I hear a haunting croon that grows in intensity. My own face continues glaring at me in the green hologram—and my own reflection—in complete horror—begins to morph into *him*—that devil with the CLAW!

That demon? No! Anyone but . . .

It is happening, that dreaded face is again before me: Lord Wolford! Laughing, mocking, every laugh like a blow to my chest, to my stomach, reopening every scar still visible on my bruised body.

My chest is beating harder and faster than ever.

"No. Go! Go away you demon! This is over!" I scream to Lord Wolford, the one I hate. But the louder I scream, the harder he laughs while his aqua eyes gleam through the crystal.

"Doorman!"

I try to get up, but I'm stuck—frozen stiff, trapped inside my own body. Completely immobilized. Every limb melts like putty. My eyes freeze like a spectator forced to keep watching a horror I do not want to see a second time around. My only concern is getting out of this cell, just getting free. "Go away! Go!" I plead.

Overtaken, a low, painful groan wells up from deep within my chest. Louder and louder it raises until I'm shouting, "My elixir! Doorman! My elixir NOW!" I scream. But no one comes. "Help! Doorman! Please just one more dose!"

I can do nothing. And then, everything around me goes black, and all I can see is this nightmarish phantasma as if I'm inside of it myself, reliving every detail, stepping into a dead story I had closed the book on.

If I could just get out of this prison, then I could forget. I'm left shaking and cold in this tiny concrete hole that smells like a mix of mold and ashes—with nothing but this green stone. *Is this some kind of hex? It's like a witch stirring a cauldron of snakes around me.*

"Doorman! DOOOORMAAAN! My ELLLIIIXER!"

Then, after an interval of more pleads and screams, I try to scream again but the sound is like a groan from the bottom of my soul when the feelings are too deep to articulate or mutter. And then, my stomach seems to rise into my throat as the green light swallows me, and I am thrust into the horrific nightmare—cast by this mysterious, horrendous, ghoulish green stone . . .

CHAPTER TWO

PAST
8 YEARS OLD

Valley of Dry Bones

I was eight years old.

Who is this man? What does he want? What is he going to do to me?

His claw covered my mouth. I couldn't scream. He scooped me up like a rag doll. Every beat from my heart pounded in terror. He caged my screams in his large hands—carrying me by foot. My senses felt so alive. Quickly—hushed—sharply! He whirled me into the forest by moonlight.

"Shh. It won't be long," he whispered. His voice kept hissing in my ear like a snake slithering in warm, green grass. "You are mine now, Sunbeam."

Sunbeam? My twin. Why was he calling me Sunbeam?

I clutched the locket dangling on my chest that Sunbeam had given me. The golden locket glinted under the moon. *Who is this man? What is he going to do to me?* This was the terrifying tape playing over and over in my mind. And even more, why did I agree to play Sunbeam's stupid game? Was this all part of her game? Was she up to this? Well, it wasn't funny! She'd gone too far!

When he carried me, I could barely contain my feelings but kept completely quiet. I couldn't even think a complete thought, much less talk. Driven by a mix of fear and curiosity, I looked up at him. Why did I want to see his face? Maybe I hoped it would look less horrific than I imagined. I glanced, but he was wearing a mask. Through the two eyeholes of it, I could see only his blue eyes sparkling like ice under the moon. His eyes. So brilliant blue—but so evil. Was there a speck of kindness somewhere in them? I looked deeper into those mysterious marbles as they gleamed, hoping for some semblance of decency, but saw an aquamarine of relentless rage.

"Shh! It will be over soon!" He whispered, but this time in a tone that carried an intent to warn rather than soothe.

After a long stretch through trees and river, we came to the opening of a cave.

"Not much longer," he whispered.

At the entry of the cave, I started to tremble. For I was looking into an abyss of blackness with no end. I couldn't utter a sound because my heart was beating so fast my throat felt tight—and then—we entered.

Through much strain, my voice escaped and burst from my hammering chest. "No-o-o-!" I screamed. It echoed through the cave. "Where are you taking me? Who are you? Don't hurt me! Please! Don't hurt me!"

I started kicking my legs. I swung my arms trying to injure him. But he tightened his grip and smirked. His strength overpowered me. Through the stone halls of the cave, he stepped with intent through twists and turns until he sat me down in pitch blackness. In the next moment, he struck a match. The flame flickered as he lit a lantern. Shadows danced on the curves of his face. His eyes gleamed down. Then, I felt the extent of his power as he bound me with chains around my ankles and coiled them up to my wrists. *Who are you? Why?* I thought. *What is he planning? What's this demon going to do to me?* I quickly dismissed the many horrid possibilities just as soon as they presented themselves.

"Please! Don't . . . don't hurt me." My lip quivered and I started to cry. And my thoughts ran and ran like a blasting faucet. I tried to shut them off, but they just kept pouring. *What would he do? Why me? Was Sunbeam in on this? Will she come out laughing "It was just a joke Gilda! Just a joke!" Or was this real and—was he going to kill me?*

Then suddenly, he froze and glared at me with his cold eyes. Everything went silent, a silence that chilled me to the bone. And I became too terrified to keep crying. He'd chained me so tight my body sat still on the outside but shook wildly on the inside. My chest hammered so hard, the chain-links bounced back and forth on my chest. I gasped for quick, short breaths. "Pl . . . Pleas—" I muttered—"just don't . . ."

"Hush, child," he said. He turned sharply and whipped around, so I saw only the back of his head. He leaned against the wall of the cave in deep thought. Then with the light of the lantern, I watched him pace like a wild animal back and forth in the half-light. Only the sound of his growling breath filled the air. And I grew more furious every time he hissed, "Sunbeam," for I was NOT Sunbeam! But my instinct told me not to utter this fact, for my life depended on it.

"Sunbeam," he said with a low groan, "it is here you will contemplate your fate."

"What? What does that mean? Wha . . ." I cried.

"You are the One Called, Sunbeam. And with that comes benefits, but also consequences." He snarled. His sharp teeth showed themselves when his lip slightly curled.

And it was in that moment the truth rained down on me; the only reason I was in this terrible condition was because I agreed to play that game Sunbeam made me play. To trick our new nanny on who was who. I was sleeping in Sunbeam's bed, and she, in mine, to see if the new nanny could tell us apart. So, he had taken the wrong twin. I was Gilda, not Sunbeam! But the game had gone too far! I looked around. *Oh please, Sunbeam! You can jump out laughing now. Tell me this is all part of the game!*

"What do we have here?" He leaned in closer and studied the golden locket on my chest—of which Sunbeam wore the other half. He reached over and ripped it from my neck. "Collateral," he smirked. He closed my locket tightly into his fist.

"Give that back!" I shouted. I felt a hot fire shoot through my eyes—anger darkened my senses.

Then as he bent down to lock my chains, with that loud SNAP! of the lock, my heart swelled with fiery coldness. For even though I loved my sister, this would be the very last time Sunbeam's tricks would injure me.

CHAPTER THREE

PRESENT
13 YEARS OLD

Holding cell, Realm of the Dark Night

"Ahhhh! Nooo!" My heart skips a beat. The witchy-green portal of the crystal swallows itself up. I wake, sweating from the past nightmare, faced with the reality I'm still trapped in this cell. Everything is dark again. *After all this time, I still don't know how I got here. I suspect it's Wolford who put me here. Or Sunbeam? I can't pin it! And now this cryptic stone?*

Every time I wake from one of these feverish nightmares, I see *him* crouched in the corner, laughing at me, sharpening his claw. Yes, I am still a prisoner, but my prison isn't this cell; it's my own thoughts that lock me up. I hate him. Hate, hate, hate! All this time, and he won't leave me alone. *Have I lost my mind? Certainly, I have not. He wronged me. Even more, my beloved Sunbeam had wronged me all the more.* I clutch the stone and throw it as hard as I can against the wall. "Damn you!" But it won't break. And suddenly, like that serpent stone, I realize that to survive I must move on, hard-hearted and unbreakable. I have no choice—covered with dirt and scars on the outside, I'm tired, and my clothes are torn up and my black hair is caked with dirt and ragged—just like my soul.

"Doorman?" I take a chance and call out once more. My elixir helps me when my thoughts feel jumbled, when my heart is a tornado. But they took my drug away. Ever since, I'm starting to feel all the dreadful things that I forgot. Surprisingly, that's the one thing the demon gave me that meant anything at all: elixir. *It'll numb the pain,* he'd say.

So, yes. You could say I'm damaged.

GILDA: THE LOST TWIN

CHAPTER FOUR

LORD WOLFORD

PRESENT

To: The Guild of Golgums

Subjects,

It has come to my attention that Gilda has been placed in a holding cell—imprisoned in the Realm of Dark Night. At the end of her sentence, she will either fly up to the light, to that sanctuary I loathe, or be cast down for eternity—back to our realm.

Hundreds of injuries have kept her stuck. We still have time, but it is urgent. If she does get out of that cell and enters His domain, the fight is over. We will lose her. We are prohibited beyond that boundary.

As you know, we are forbidden to enter her cell physically in that sphere, but we can disturb activity through other paranormal forces. The mind is its own domain and can make a heaven out of hell, and a hell out of heaven. Through these other forces we will fight for equal ground.

Before Gilda can go forward, she must first go back and conquer her past. Until then, she will remain in the holding cell. It is in the law.

Indeed, it is in her reliving all the events of her past that we will take hold at present, and through subtle entry, reclaim her.

Gilda is in a terrible condition. We still have time. She has tasted our world. And once formerly had, captives are easy to reclaim.

Your Prince,

LORD WOLFORD

GILDA: THE LOST TWIN

CHAPTER FIVE

GILDA

PRESENT
13 YEARS OLD

Holding cell, Realm of the Dark Night

I'm still lying on my back—on this cold, cell floor. Who knows how long I've been wasting in this wet prison. I've never adapted to the coldness, the dampness. My long, black hair is sticky and matted. I used to be a natural blonde until the charms of witchery turned it to the color of a crow's wing. My eyes, green by birth, have stayed the same, except for when I transform: they glow deeper, like the pit of an olive.

Rage rushes through me. *Am I just supposed to die here?* Driven by the storm in my chest, I sit up. I reach for my elixir, but it's not here. I reach further, but my hands feel nothing but cold air. *Nothing? Wait—I don't have it anymore. How can I live without it? Ahh! If I can get through one day without it, I can quit it altogether. One more day, one more day . . .* is the tape playing over in my head. *One more day . . .* that's what the doorman said after they weaned me off it.

Bruises cover my back and legs from convulsing on the hard floor when I don't have my drug. But to my relief, the hardest part of withdrawal is over now since it's out of my bloodstream. My feet are filthy, fingernails caked with guck and dirt. I haven't had any real food in years, just the sludge they slide through my door's window slot. I miss the delicious hot soup, breads, and sweets I would eat at home. Now that was real living! I pinch myself to make sure I'm still alive: this nightmare has become my reality. But reality feels so far away.

The days have all run together: Weeks. Months. Years.

I'm locked in this dark sea—still drowning in a whirl of fragmented memories. They won't let me out of this cell, not even to use the bathroom. At least they're decent enough to have a stall in here.

I assume the outside world is terrified of me. Why? Because many dabble in dark magic like kids trying a new sport, but some are either killed by their own sorcery or run the opposite way from the nightmares they uncage. Not me. I have mastered it. Darkness bows at my feet.

I squeeze my crystal. The light glints, calling up another memory. . . .

CHAPTER SIX

GILDA

PAST
YEARS AGO

Valley of Dry Bones

I remember it all too well, being a captive back in Wolford's dungeon. It had been years since he stole me from my bed. Wolford's minions had made a habit of mocking me, jealous of Wolford's regard for my gift.

"The master claims you have powers. Show us! Prove it!" They'd mock. "He tells the guild you're a seer! Uh-huh! The only thing we see is your dirty face! Ha Ha!" They roared in laughter, pointing their large bony fingers at me. Suddenly, the mouthiest one stepped forward, "Well, I wouldn't go betting on it! Look at her!"

The others stood behind him, clapping their big, sharp teeth in laughter. "That's right! Prove your power! Call forth a rat! So we may have it for dinner!"

"That's right! That's right!" The others behind him scoffed. Their bones rattled as they shuffled around me.

"Vile pigs! Quiet! Or I'll show you who I am!" I raised my fist. "I'll crack those big hardheads of yours in two!"

Hesitantly, the golgums scuttled back against the wall, peering through their hollow, stubborn sockets. Those bony nothings were mere distractions. Little did they know I had bigger things to contend with.

I picked up the *Book of Shadows* that Wolford gave me, which always lay in my chamber. "Stay back," I warned. In the next moment, I opened the ancient book. And a dark mist rose from its pages. "Are you ready?" I asked.

"Uh-huh! Prove it! Or we'll rush upon you and have YOU for dinner—dirty face!" They smirked and shuffled.

"OK, dimwits! A rat you want? A rat you will get." I raised my hands on each side like wings. The pages ruffled, growing in intensity until there came a dark wind, twisting into a pillar of smoke. My eyes burned and began glowing green, which sent two sharp beams against the wall. At once, I spoke. My voice echoed so loudly, it vibrated the chamber walls.

"With a lizard tail and slyness of a cat,
I call from the depths,
a massive, venomous RAT!"

The smoke thickened.

"Oh! You've really done it this time! Why'd you ask her to prove it?" cried one of the golgums to the other.

"Stop your whining!" the other snapped back. Then they all went to choking, for the smoke had smothered the whole dungeon until—lo and behold—their coughing was replaced with a screeching sound that pierced the whole chamber. "REEER!" it shrieked. "REEEER!" And when the smoke disappeared, a horrifying creature with the body of a rat, the tail of a lizard, and hissing face of a cat manifested in my cloud of sorcery. The golgums gasped in horror.

I continued:

"Oh, sweet kitty,
A rat for dinner these hardheads begged,

And dinner they shall have,
Lest first, you have their heads!"

The hideous rat creature bared its fangs and licked its chops. "REEER!" It swiveled its head, then froze, locking its beady eyes on the golgums, whose taunting smirks transformed and stretched back in sheer terror. With their backs against the wall, they began to bicker among themselves in jumbles of "The master told you not to!" "Look what you've done!" "You did it!" "No, you did it!" "The master will flog you for this!" They argued.

"REEEER!" The feline-rat crept toward them while foam dripped down its fangs.

"There kitty-kitty! Have some food." I grinned.

Then the boldest golgum turned to me and pleaded, "Please! We only teased! A mere jest! Ha! Call it back. Call it back! Ha Ha!" They chuckled through shaky voices while raising their bony hands to guard themselves. The rat creature, only inches from them, snarled. I continued my spell:

"Creature of the valley, they called you for dinner,
let us see who will eat,
and come out the winner!
For the vileness they wished upon you,
to them—
you shall turn and do!"

In the next second, the boldest golgum leapt toward me, followed by a mix of "Slay her!" "Tear her to pieces!" "Bring her to the master!"

A ball of chaos broke out through the dungeon. The feline-rat had leapt and was streaking across the chamber like grey lightning. There was nothing but fangs, hissing, fur and bones crashing in the dungeon. Then the boldest golgum broke from the bustle and latched onto my ankle like a mad dog, trying to tear my flesh.

"Get! You maggot!" I snapped and pulled my leg back with great force, kicking it against the stone wall. This loosened its grip from my ankle. It fell on its bony back, flailing and gnashing its teeth to bite my legs, screeching, "To the master! Bring her to the master!"

"I've tussled with things with twice the fight you've got!" I snapped, and in a flash—WHOP!—brought down my fist on top of its large head, which shattered it into a heap of bones.

"REEEER!" The feline-rat shrieked. I looked up to find the other golgums fleeing on foot; the rat creature's large lizard tail flailed as it chased them out of my chamber. "You did this fool!" "No, you did it, lunkhead!" "We'll get her! We'll tell the master!" The golgums' voices bickered down the hall.

"Enjoy, kitty-kitty!" I chuckled. The creature growled after them, until I heard their terrified footsteps vanish deep down the tunnels of the cave.

I assume word spread through the valley after that. For not many in the depths dared to cross me.

CHAPTER SEVEN

PRESENT
13 YEARS OLD

Holding cell, Realm of the Dark Night

Snapping back to reality, the green portal of the past fades. I'm still locked up in this damn cell. If only I had the *Book of Shadows*. There was never a mystery the ancient spell book couldn't help me solve. If I had it, I could escape this prison, make that doorman run like the dimwit golgums. The book is the only valuable thing I got from him: my captor, the one I hate. The one who bore me a thousand injuries, yet the one who opened the book of black magic for me. *And that claw, that awful claw. Never again.*

"You are a seer, child," Lord Wolford would say. "But remember, I am the one who discovered you first."

I'm *limited* inside this cell. I have my spells, but I can't transcend beyond the bars. I can't astral travel across ethereal planes. I am stuck. I need more.

I want freedom. *Real* freedom.

I gaze at my green, serpentine crystal. It's all I have. This stone is mine now, and it's becoming a comfort of sorts. I've been ruminating on this stone for weeks. I am a seer. *Dark magic is the best revenge,* I think to myself. *I have seen the evidence of black magic, which the one with the claw performed on his victims.*

This stone is serpentine. It's the hardest stone to break due to its perfect schism in three dimensions. I clutch it tightly. So far, this crystal hasn't let me down. Since it first appeared in my cell weeks ago, it's begun to grow on me. I mean, it's the only solid thing I have. I tear a string of twine from my straw mat and loop it as a charm around my neck. The crystal dangles from my necklace, reliably on my chest. Oh, the last necklace I treasured was the one Sunbeam gave me: the golden heart locket that Wolford ripped from my neck the night he stole me. Sunbeam and I had just eaten a whole bag of pastel colored candy under a tree. And her lips were pink as the sunset when she kissed my cheek and said, "Our lockets fit like a puzzle." She lifted her half to mine, and it formed a whole heart. "We'll always be together," she promised. She smiled sweetly and hugged me. I wonder if she still wears her half? But that time is over, an old memory that once meant a lot to me.

I clutch my new necklace now. "Show me. Help me." I talk to it. I sense it hears me. This stone is precious. I feel it wants to open an old door to a realm I buried long ago, but one I must reenter. It's been reminding me of my past, and even more, giving me glints of my future. I squeeze it tighter. "You know time is running out. You won't let me down," I whisper to it.

In the next moment, I fumble for my elixir again. "Doorman!" I scream. "My elixir!" There is no reply. "Doorman, NOW!" Still, no reply.

Long silence . . .

I begin to sweat. I want my drug. Swooning, I lie back down. *If I can get through one day without it, I can quit altogether. One more day . . . one more day . . .* plays the mantra in my head. I know the answer is just beyond my reach. I must unlock my prison, or I'll be stuck in this hellhole forever like a hardened mummy in a forgotten tomb—frozen forever in a place I don't belong, with nothing but a collection of bad memories while everyone else's life goes on.

I sense my fate is drawing near. The cell shrinks smaller and smaller. The walls and ceiling now wrap around closer than ever. Laughing. Taunting. A slow torment toward my crushing death. *Who put me here? And why? Wolford? Sunbeam?*

Revenge is mine. I clutch my serpentine. I can't die here. Or am I already dead? Is my silver cord cut?

I will figure out an escape. And at this point, now that all else has failed, and how wrong—and how deeply they have injured me—I contemplate doing the worst crime. The stone whispers of spilling blood, but whose blood shall I spill?

In a second, the noise of a quick footstep alerts me. I hear its slight movement on the other side of my chamber door. I creep across the cell—stealthily as a cat, completely quiet. I raise my ear and press it against the door. I sense a presence on the other side—and remain completely still for many minutes. "Who's there?" I whisper.

Silence.

Could it be the doorman? It didn't matter anyway because he wouldn't be bringing my elixir. I hadn't had a drop of it in weeks . . . months . . . it was all-out agony! And all the feelings I had numbed were growing into an unbearable hurricane in my chest. But surprisingly, I was somehow managing to ride out this storm without it. Besides, I have this stone now; it's a sort of comfort.

Suddenly, the metal window slot on my door creaks. Someone is sliding it open! "Who's there?" No reply. The slot barely opens, leaving a tiny slice of light breaking through. *What on earth?*

Dim candlelight flickers through the open slither. "Who's there?" Then, the door slot opens a little wider until an obscure, shadowed face is peering through it.

"I . . . I didn't mean to scare you, Miss Gilda?" says the figure. The voice is strong and smooth, and overly polite. I can't make out the features of the face, just a shadowy profile. And by the curve of it, I know it's NOT the doorman.

"Yes, I am Gilda."

"Oh, Miss Gilda."

"Yes?" I ask. "Who are you? Where is the doorman?" *No one other than the doorman has ever come to my door.*

"Uhh . . . the old one is . . . has . . . retired." He brings the candle closer to his face, so I can see a courteous smile in the flicker. I sense something familiar about him.

"Retired . . . why?"

"He was dumb as a dog!" he spurts.

Then, as if holding back a strong overflow of feelings, he inhales deeply, and I can hear him swallow hard in the dark. He takes another deep breath. "There must be something I can offer you," he says.

I can do nothing but study this dim-lit figure, this talking silhouette.

"Look at you. You must be starving," he says. "Any pleasures I can bring you? Or, abominations?" He chuckles in jest, but with a seriousness in his tone, as if he has the power to give me anything I want.

I haven't had any elixir in a good while. I think to myself. *Can I trust him? Do I want it after all this time? Water instead? Food? I'm starving! The elixir would be nice—no—I'll have to start over at step one and the convulsions and the dizziness and . . . . Ahhh!* My thoughts run into one wild stream, pouring out all at once.

"There must be something . . . something I can offer you?" the voice says.

I know that voice, but from where? "Well . . . well there *is* something . . . but the doorman wouldn't give—"

“The other doorman was a careless fool,” he says. “He wasn’t doing his job.”

Why is he being so nice? Can I trust him? My thoughts spiral.

He asks again, “Some . . . elixir?” Eager to please, there’s a zeal in his deep voice.

“What?” I blurt. *How on earth does he know about my elixir? Did the other doorman leave him instructions?* “Well . . . uh . . . uhhh . . . I . . . yah . . . yah, sure,” I mutter aloud before I can think.

“Settle now, my dear. You needn’t be reluctant to ask for exactly what you desire.” With that, he briskly turns his silhouetted profile toward the hallway and slides the door slot shut. And I hear his footsteps march hurriedly down the corridor to fetch the abomination, as he joked, for which I craved.

And as I waited for my drug, Serpentine alights. “No. No, not NOW!” I say. “Nooo!” I’m left clutching my crystal, the spooky, green glimmer slowly swallows me once again into that dreadful portal of my past.

CHAPTER EIGHT

GILDA

PAST
YEARS AGO

Valley of Dry Bones

I was too young the first time I tasted the drug: the elixir. It had been years in Wolford's underworld, since the night he stole me from Sunbeam's bed. Night after night, he'd hold the cup of elixir to my lips. The smell of it filled my nose. It smelled like a crushed leaf mixed with gasoline. Each time I smelled it, my stomach winced. I'd always draw back to decline. But like clockwork, again and again, he'd hold it to my lips before the night hours. He never stopped.

"My child, look at you. Such sullen, angry eyes. Drink," he'd say.

"No. Please," I begged. "Just let me go. Get me out of this hell."

"My dear, Sunbeam, just as smoke hurts the eyes, so your memories disturb your sight," Wolford said. "You are the One Called. You require a clearer field of vision than others." His eyes looked like a wolf, reflecting the torch of an angry, blue fire. What's more, he still thought I was Sunbeam. And for years, I lay chained to a lie—lying to Wolford—the father of all lies.

"You are almost of age, child. You will decide for yourself whom you will serve. Him—or me."

"Him? Who's this HIM you speak of?"

"He is the one who wakes the dead," he snarled. "But child, do not concern yourself with Him because not all the dead wake up, nor will you or I know what time he will come." He stared off for a moment, as if hesitant, then snapped back and bared his fangs. "Drink this cup! It will clear that smoke from your dingy eyes and melt away those memories on which you dwell."

He held the cup to my lips. For a brief moment, his talk of relief enticed my turbulent mind. I considered accepting. "Maybe just one . . . one sip . . ." my lips quivered on the rim of the cup. *Maybe it will help me feel better for the night, just one night? No. No, no no! This devil offers nothing except what's devilish.*

"Drink, child. Drink. Your mind is a treacherous storm. This will calm those raging waters."

He leaned in closer. His eyes, only an inch from my own, stared down into my soul. Then to my surprise, his eyes softened. And even though I knew he was a devil, for a split moment, I could see there might have been some good in him, long ago. As a seer, I didn't miss the sudden change of his face. And maybe this shred of goodness in him wanted to pull out this blade he drove in my heart. And even more—the blade Sunbeam twisted in my heart every day I thought about her stupid game! And in that moment, something started overtaking my soul and I . . . I took a sip of the drink, but then I spit it right out in his devil face. "Anything you offer is hell! Now, get out of my chamber! Black-hearted swine!"

And before I could even think or know what I said, I had already said it. And it was the very first time I'd stood up to him. But in the next second, I immediately shrunk back against the wall and put up my hands to guard my face. I mean, what did I just do? What on earth came over me? I didn't know if he'd slap me, kick me, kill me, or what. And for what seemed like eternity, my words hung in the silence—with that wretched elixir I spit on him, dripping down his face. His eyebrows raised in shock. His expression was frozen, yet he seemed on the verge of striking like a startled snake that had just been stepped on.

My heart pounded like a hammer, not knowing if this would be the end of me until he broke the long silence with devilish laughter, which started as a faint hiss until it grew into robust bellows. He roared in hisses and growly cackles, baring his fangs. Then in an instant, like a snake, he coiled down within an inch of my face, and hissed, "Angry, are you? There it is! There is the fire I have waited to stir. All this time, you've lain here chained like a dog, weak and whipped. Your soul must be *very* deep, child. It's taken this long to arouse that flame, but now, I see you've been stirred to the depths." He stepped closer to me and traced the tip of his claw into a heart-shape over my chest. "Only fools and weaklings keep their hearts tranquil when their impulses call for blood and justice."

"Release me, Wolford. I want to go home," I demanded.

"Dear Sunbeam," he smirked, "you have every right to be angry. But had you not lain here sheltered in evil, that evil would still have found you out there in the world. And you would be angry with someone or something else. Think of this as training."

"Training? For what?"

"For when I unleash you. All those people who deserve death and all the wrongs they have committed. Being sheltered in evil will help you defeat the evil out there. An eye for an eye. That's what it takes to win. Lambs do not defeat wolves. Only wolves defeat wolves."

"Leave me. Just go. GO!" I shouted.

"That's it. Let it out, child. I know your fury burns deep."

"DEVIL! GET THE HELL OUT OF HERE!" I began to shout so loudly and so forcibly I thought I would faint. But what's more, he still didn't know who I was—I was Gilda—not Sunbeam. And this enraged me even more. *She* should have been the one locked up, *not me*. She should be chained in the consequences of her dumb game she forced me to play, switching identities. Not even a glimpse of her since, despite me holding sweet visions of our life together and the love I'd held in my heart, which faded more each day I sat in that dank dungeon of hell.

"Let me out of here! Now! I'll kill you!" Electric strength surged down my body. In a second, before I could think, I was soaring across the chamber and kicked Wolford in the center of his chest—THWAP!—which sent him flying hard against the wall. In a flash, I pinned him to the ground. With me over him, that surge grew stronger down my arms; I struck him in the face which sent a splatter of blood against the wall.

"Settle down!" he commanded. He grabbed my arms, whirled over me, and jumped back to his feet. He seized both of my wrists, cupped them in his large hand, and pulled me across the chamber. "Go back to where you belong! Until you learn to hear and obey!" Then he threw me to the ground and held up the chains.

"No! Not the chains! Not again!" I screamed.

"To hear is to obey, child!" he hissed. He bound me tightly—and locked the key.

"Unchain me! You vile maggot! Old bag-of-beast!" I yelled more obscenities for what seemed like forever. Wolford stood up tall and pulled a torch from the sconce. His lips turned upward into a mischievous grin. *What's he going to do?* I froze, dismissing all the horrid possibilities. Suddenly, he began to dance madly, yet elegantly. His nose was in the air like a pompous prince—gliding—with each dance step, he began to provoke and jab at my flesh with the torch flame.

"Stop! It's burning me. Stop!" I pleaded. But in my distress, that fiend only danced and jabbed me even more with his fire, hissing in exultation—until I dropped my shoulders, too weary to keep fighting. And after more twirling and dancing with his torch flame, he came to a halt. In the next second, he glided madly toward me. And by this point, I was too tired to even cry or be afraid. He stood, looking down on me with his flame an inch from my flesh, so scalding hot that I turned completely cold.

He knelt, and for the millionth time, held the elixir to my lips: the drug he promised would ease my pain.

"Your soul is a deep abyss of disturbed waters," he said, "and this will take the focus from it. There, there, let your heart be tranquil. Drink, child." He spoke gently.

"Please, just go away," I muttered.

"Well, child, you force me to help you the hard way." He grabbed my hand. "Take it," he urged. He squeezed it so tightly I thought it would break.

"Please, leave me alone. Pleeeease!"

Then, he tightened his grip with his claw around my finger and—SNAP!—broke my finger at the joint.

"OWWWW! You devil!" I was minutes from fainting.

"Since you won't drink the remedy I offer, I have just done you a favor. External gashes are easier to bear than internal wounds. This, child, you will learn." He put the drug to my nose. I hated the smell of it.

"And this, dear Sunbeam, will numb all those wounds, so you can complete the work." He smiled. "Tonight, you will lie in darkness, and enable the greater sights to manifest." He picked up the *Book of Shadows* and placed it next to me. "You may not be where you want to be, little girl, but you must be willing to have visions that will lead you to a proud and glorious end!"

Then in all his cruelness, he took my other hand and began to squeeze it, too.

"No! Please. No!" I begged and tried to pull away. If I weren't chained, I'd have slayed him.

"If you are trusty and well-behaved and prove to your prince, full power will be yours to prevent your own bloodshed, and in the wars levying in the realm of the gods, you will take dominion in spilling the blood of others." His blue eyes gleamed wildly. "You will use this gift to bring justice. Drink," he commanded. "Drink!"

What will this stuff do? What if it's poison? My heart raced.

"Drink. I'm about to do you another favor," he grimaced, ready to snap my other finger. And before I could even think, fainting with a broken finger and bleeding heart, I grabbed the cup—and I . . . I DRANK IT! And in the next second, something happened I couldn't believe. A wave of intense relief washed over me. I sank back in a cloud of ecstasy while my broken finger bled almost as badly as my broken heart. But strangely, the drink comforted my heart too, like a magical tonic.

"See, my child—euphoria. Ease your pain. This is what the elixir will do!" He smiled and stroked my hair. And I hated him with every fiber inside of me, but surprisingly, even the wild hate I felt for that demon began to subside as the elixir washed through my veins. I took another drink.

He picked up the *Book of Shadows* and held it in the air like a prized trophy. He opened it. And with the tip of his claw, pointed to a line on the dusty page. "Now, read this line out loud," he commanded.

I leaned in and read it aloud: "A fiery star is born in dust, and in the pressure of darkness."

He smiled dangerously at me. "Be careful, child, these pages are filled with the darkest of magic." He cupped my chin with his claw. His touch felt hot like fire but chilled me.

After a moment, he set down the book, along with the cup of elixir, next to my chains. He glared into my eyes, studying my face, until he took the flaming torch and turned away. In the firelight, as he marched out, I saw only his shadow on the dungeon wall until he faded away into the tunnel.

I was left chained with nothing but thoughts. I took another drink of the elixir and thumbed through the book. I was still learning its spells and chapters. I had performed magic before, but there was more to learn. Exploring more of its tattered, archaic pages—it was full of images and ancient writings that I could somehow see and understand. I flipped and flipped until my eyes fell upon something that caught my attention. *What is this?* I smeared away the dust to unveil more lines and features of the sketch, which bore the face of a man. And it was then my heart leaped, and everything went silent. It was HIM! The man of light I'd seen as child! Oh, could it really be him? Why was he in the *Book of Shadows*? *What in the name of* . . . I leaned in to study the face closely. The caption underneath his face read:

The Lamb,
Crusher of our light,
He outshines our truth,
He destroys all sorcerous nights.
His hallowed fire burns up magical chaff,
His power swallows wizardry staffs.
Your secret arts and silver, if you want to keep,
See and flee—this great ENEMY.

And suddenly, sitting in that pit of hell, I looked down at the palm of my hand onto the tiny scar, still imprinted from that seed he planted in my hand when I was a lost child. *Is this the same man?* And suddenly, the tiny scar pulsed gold. *What on earth?* Then his voice resonated inside of me like a peaceful stream, as it did when I was small: *When lost in the dark, know the sun will rise soon.*

And wondering what it all meant, and so many questions left unanswered—with a broken finger and bleeding heart, I slammed the book shut.

CHAPTER NINE

LORD WOLFORD

PRESENT

My Loyal Abaddon,

I trust you are now with Gilda. Do not be a fool. Manage her well. Poor, desperate girl. Her weakness is no different than a street prostitute's. She would sell anything for the things she loves and hates altogether.

She is not able to turn away all the enticements of the present moment. It is through the elixir we will take hold, and through this entry, rouse deeper resentments. Her soul is confused and dithers in its calculations.

Remember, dear Abaddon, you must ask. We can neither enter through her door, nor give anything to which she has not first consented. This way, it's her choice, and she bears the guilt of her own doing, and undoing. We can stand at the door, but she must choose to let us in.

Do not worry, but rather, marvel at the simpleness of these matters. Her desperate state will lead to pleasures enjoyed now, which will take her eye off eternity.

Do not tarry, for I assume HE will be coming soon—to her rescue.

Your Prince,

LORD WOLFORD

CHAPTER TEN

GIL'DA

PRESENT
13 YEARS OLD

Holding cell, Realm of the Dark Night

Tonight is the night. I sense it. What's coming feels like both joy and terror, and I don't know which one will win. With this new doorman, whoever he is, at least I know one thing—I can escape for one night if he brings my drug.

It feels like hours since he left my chamber. So, I wait at the mercy of when he decides to return. *Who is he? What happened to the other one? Be cautious Gilda! You know the wound of treachery—it pierces trust in one cut. There's something about him . . . something familiar.*

My thoughts run as I consider his demeanor, his obscure shadow in the half-light. For once, someone decent in this lonely, barren place of punishment—dark, with no color, no trees or rivers, completely cheerless and dull with nothing but cell rock. Anything! Any semblance of kindness would brighten this prison. I lie back down and take my place in a bed of hopelessness, with nothing but green and grime on the ceiling to blanket me. I clutch my stone. *How did I end up like this?* I just want to sleep for a thousand years.

"This place has a way of silencing you," a voice fills the room. It's him: the new doorman!

What . . . ? He came so quietly! I didn't know he was there; or had he been standing there all long? My eyes search the darkness to find him peering through the metal slot where they shove gunk called food through my door. Only the corner of his mouth and chiseled chin are visible in the square window slot—dimly lit by his flickering candle.

"Oh . . . you! You startled me," I sit up, heart racing because you see it was scarcely, if ever, someone checked on me in the midnight hours. And now, here is this figure, speaking to me in pitch blackness with searching eyes and a smooth, affectionate tone.

"May I open the door?"

Open my door? Is he dangerous? Why all this attention? The other doorman has NEVER entered. He only ever stuck his head through the slot to scan the cell and make sure I was still alive with his, "Very good. Very good," then slam it shut.

"Umm, that is fine," I mutter. I brace, ready to defend myself if needed.

Then, very cautiously, he twists the handle. The door creaks as it widens. A tall, dark figure stands at the threshold. His body fills the entire doorway, and the whites of his eyes scan the four corners of my cell, carefully, as if checking for some intruder. He attempts to cross the threshold into my cell but abruptly stops, as if he's just seen a snake. Quickly, he brings his foot back and remains across the boundary line of my door.

Now a little closer, and in the light of his lantern, I take in his countenance. He looks much younger than the previous doorman, maybe nineteen or twenty-something. He has long, dark brown hair that hangs to his shoulders. His eyes are deep-set and so dark they look black and bottomless, as if carrying many mysteries beneath them. His body is tall and sinewy, cut and chiseled, like some Greek god. Although his skin is pale, it's smooth and highlights his dark features. He straightens his collar and smiles.

"How are you feeling, Miss Gilda?" His dark eyes sparkle, as if eager to please me, gleaming in the firelight of a blue flame, from some strange candle he holds in his hand—and in the other hand—a chalice that contains my elixir. He starts to enter my cell but stops abruptly—freezes—and swallows like a wild animal lying in wait for its food. My heart thumps harder. I attempt to break the uncomfortable tension filling my chamber.

"I . . . I see you've brought my elixir?"

His feet remain cemented at the doorsill, firm, careful not to cross the line.

Long silence.

"I . . . I've never seen a candle like that. That flame . . . ," I blurt among the thickness of the tension growing in the cell. But while I'm looking at the flame that flickers blue and cold, I'm craving my drink. I don't want small talk, just the drink—then for him to go.

"Yes, Miss Gilda. These candles," he says, smiling, "are said to reflect how the one who looks at its flame feels on the inside. What color does the fire look to you?" He chuckles lightly, as if performing a magic trick.

"Blue."

"Blue?" His eyes narrow in thought. "Well, blue is the warmest color."

"Yes, or the coldest," I smirk.

"Oh, yes, well enough of that. Miss Gilda, I have brought what you asked." His voice becomes empathic, as if ready to give me relief for an open wound.

He stands holding the chalice. My drug swirls inside of it. Suddenly, I catch a faint smell of it. My breath quickens. I wait patiently for him to hand it over, but he will not step across the threshold. I step closer to the open door. I don't know exactly how long I'd been without my drug. I only know every fiber inside of me craves it to the last drop. And now, I stand gazing in disbelief at the thing I've been wanting, wanting to taste, wanting what could blot out my pain in this hellish prison. *One more day. If you can get through one day without it, you can quit altogether. Wait, should I . . . ?* Trembling, and against all better judgement, I open my hand.

He holds up the cup, "My dear, never hesitate to ask for what you desire." I reach for the cup. He jerks it backward, "And in this case, what appears you absolutely *need*."

Then, he extends his arm to hand me the drink. My thoughts race. *One more day . . . one more day . . . Ahhh! Yes! No! I should not! I . . .*

I take it.

Now in my hand, it floods my senses—the most glorious scent—the smell, indescribable but disastrously beautiful and distinct causes exhilaration to flow through me. At this point, I'm done entertaining him. I want to drink—and for him to go.

"That will be all. Thank you."

"My pleasure," he stands, waiting for me to take a sip.

He doesn't take the hint. He stands brazenly at my door, as if he has the right to be there. The awkward silence hangs in the air, until he finally breaks it with, "Miss Gilda, I know your name, but funny, you've never thought to ask mine."

I never thought because I don't care. OK, be nice, Gilda. You DO care about what he has to bring, don't you? You do care about this person helping you break out of this prison.

"Well, what is it?" I ask, concealing my impatience.

"Abaddon." He flashes me a wide grin.

"Well, thank you, Abaddon." He remains at my door. "Thank you!" I repeat in a dismissive tone.

"Oh, yes, of course—it is late." He grins and turns to leave, then peeks only his head through the slice of open door, and before he creaks it to a close, I catch the blue flame gleaming in his dark eyes.

Finally! Now holding my drug, the strong exhilaration grows in intensity. I raise the glass to my lips, quivering in anticipation, with great zeal, and burning with a desiring coldness in my belly . . . I drink!

Within seconds, heat and ice pulse through my veins. Ahh! Goosebumps hug my skin. Relaxation flows through my mind and down the back of my neck, then over my whole body like a warm blanket, blocking out all the coldness in this prison and all the coldness there ever was before it. And "Ahhhhhh," I release an audible sigh of great relief.

In the next second, I float in a cloud of numbed comfort to my trusty stone. I fall back on the floor of my cell. "Show me." I talk to it. And with the elixir expelling the coldness inside of me, and the magical stone gleaming by my side, I'm lost in complete darkness and ecstasy. In the elation of the moment, the stone begins to swell, larger and larger, greener and eerier. It alights in all of its serpentine glory, glowing slimy green hues on the iron wall, guiding me to what I must do. Again, I'm thrust into the old nightmare I yearn to leave behind, but also the nightmare the stone shows me I must dig up and hold dear—the nightmare of which—no matter how hard I fight—I cannot let go.

CHAPTER ELEVEN

GIL'DA

PAST
YEARS AGO

Valley of Dry Bones

I started seeing things way beyond this atmosphere.

I could walk around and cast spells in my chamber, but every so often, Wolford would barge in and chain me to the wall of the cave. "You will never be completely free until you accept captivity," he'd hiss.

I knew only how much time passed for the marks I carved in the rock—one for every day captive—in complete isolation—waiting for my beloved Sunbeam to save me—to tell me the game would finally be over. I held onto the idea that maybe it was *still* a game, battled the idea, because if that were the end of it, any ray of hope would die in that fiery-cold grave. And I would have lost miserably. No. The game couldn't be over. It couldn't. So, I waited and waited, but my beloved Sunbeam never came.

We always waited for each other: like the time back in school, I got in trouble standing up for her. Some of the kids called her names at recess. "Where'd you get that horse? Looks like an ugly old donkey!" They laughed and made fun of Whitewing who was tied up outside the school. I was running late to music class, but I wasn't leaving my twin sister alone.

"Disappear, dimwits!" I ran and faced them in the play yard.

"Oh look! It's two of them!" They carried on.

"That's right." I grinned. "And we're about to double down." I pictured myself dashing to the biggest and mouthiest girl, pushing her down in the dirt. A surge electrified my mind, and my eyes burned hot. But before I could start toward her—to my shock—what I saw in my mind materialized in real life because the largest bully flew through the air and splatted face down in the dirt. She whined and ran away crying with a muddy face and scraped knee, which was a cue for the rest of them to scram. "Stay away from Sunbeam—and my horse!" I shouted after them. Then I turned to my twin. "Sunbeam, did they hurt you?" I asked.

"I'm fine. But Gilda, how did that happen? You didn't touch her, but she went flying to the ground! And why do your eyes look like that?"

"I . . . I don't know." I touched my burning eyes. "Something just . . . surged out of me."

"Uh . . . well . . . we better go. You'll be in trouble." Sunbeam smiled, glad the bullies had fled, but looked a little uneasy. "I've never seen you do that."

"What are you two doing out there?" scolded one of the instructors walking toward us. "You're late!"

"Come on, let's get to class," I said. We clasped our hands and ran, chuckling all the way back.

Those memories with my twin sister were unforgettable, but they were gone, moments that had passed by.

So, I suffered alone. The first time I felt alone, I was a small child lost in the dark, and the man who glowed had come. I thought about him. Was he out there? And was that him in the *Book of Shadows*? Was he real? I remembered his words: *Child, when in darkness, the sun will always rise.*

Oh, how I yearned to see the sun again! To hear the birds and stand under the blue sky. But in the hole, there was no light, no birds chirping, nothing but the drip-drop of the wet cave. Not one visitor, not a soul in the world besides Wolford—the one I hate—who entered my darkness, bringing more darkness.

The demon crept through the cave at midnight, purling his claw in the air, with his mad dancing and singing taunting hymns, "I will shoot through you like an arrow from a bow." He leapt on rocks along the cave, posed like a mad prince, then pirouetted, stopping only to point the sharp tip of his claw toward my heart as if shooting a target. Night after night, he woke me from the little sleep I could get.

"Please, please let me sleep," I muttered.

"Child, why sleep when darkness shines brighter than the sun?" he grimaced.

"You know nothing of the dawn, you devil! Know that I will get out of this hole—I will see the sun again. The man of light will come for me." I said it before I knew what I'd said. The words erupted out of my mouth.

Wolford's whole body stiffened. He narrowed his eyes. "You saw a man? Where?" It was the first time he looked nervous.

"Yes! And he glowed like the sun and said he'd come back." *Did I see really him? Was he real? Was I a child imagining things?* Whether he was real or not, seeing Wolford's face twist into a state of alarm spurred me on. "That's right!" I continued. "He looked like the man in the *Book of Shadows*, the enemy! And why is he labeled an enemy?"

"Oh, silly girl!" Wolford smirked. "Playing make-believe. Where is this man of light now?" He leapt on a rock with his shoulders pulled back. He raised his nose in the air and looked like a mix between a hungry lion and a cruel prince posing for a portrait. He whipped his head toward me, snarled, and crouched on the ground. And before I could blink, he was crawling toward me on all fours. Then he sat down close to me. He put his arm around me and crooned in a deep, baritone growl as if singing a cryptic lullaby. The sound of the tune made me very sleepy.

"Where is he? Will he save?
This man of light,
On HIM! You must blame,
Oh child, make *Him* pay.

"Sunbeam, it is here you will contemplate,
love or hate,
be weak like the lamb,
or be like the wolf, who devoured and ate.
Choose your fate.
Chained down—in a cage!
Prisoner of rage.

"On HIM! You should blame,
Where is he? Will he save?
It is His fault. Make *Him* pay.

"You will eat up all the sheep,
Little wolf, you've done no wrong.
O' the sting of their sins!
So blood and wrath will be
your midnight song.

"And in your broken, worn-out soul
You will unchain a vulture
upon them *all*
of fire and blood,
it's justified rage,
Let your darkness swoop,
Their debt's unpaid."

His arms cradled me. He stroked my hair as the locket Sunbeam gave me swayed on his chest. "If you ever speak of this man of light again, I will kill you," he whispered. He swallowed hard and took a deep breath. "There will be no stories of gods and of men clothed with the sun," he hissed. And with his fangs only an inch from my ear, he cupped my chin with that horrid claw. "You are mine. This prison is your home." Then he crawled backwards on all fours, glaring at me with wild, aqua eyes, until disappearing into the darkness of the cave.

He still thought I was Sunbeam. For years, I concealed the truth that I was really Gilda, lest if I didn't, I feared losing my life. So, I kept pretending to be someone I wasn't, in a lonely place with no one to share my reality, not even to myself since I had to pose as someone else and lose more and more grip of who I was.

And in that state, on the fringe of complete disassociation, I began to *see* things . . . far beyond the world, I could see. For the first time in that hole, I fell into a deep vision, seeing reality in a dream. Now at this point, you assume me mad. But I say, every account I speak is true.

The gift came upon me suddenly, like a surge enlightening my mind. My eyes burned. *This feeling . . . have I felt this before? Yes, as a child.*

The presence of this strange power grew in intensity. It felt familiar, like the surges that charged my mind when I was little or when standing up for Sunbeam and she'd say, "*Gilda, how'd you do that? Why do your eyes look like that?*" My heart skipped a beat. My chest felt icy, like a cold tornado rising; this higher sense strengthened and terrified me all at once, and it amplified in magnitude. Somehow, I knew it was something more, and I was shrinking under its power: A power that was either going to make me its victim or make me unstoppable. I tried to turn away, but the sensation tugged and overtook me then enclosed my senses. When I moved my eyes, green beams moved on the wall. *My eyes . . . glowing!* And every part of me was engulfed, until after many minutes of resistance, this strange power had won—and I was completely swept away from the cavern of the cave—into another realm. And although I was in the hole, I could sense Sunbeam beyond it.

In the vision, I saw my beloved Sunbeam. Tears streamed down Sunbeam's red face as she searched and searched for me.

I saw Whitewing. He had lost the spring in his gallop, and for a horse that was very sad. He resorted to his stall, only coming out if forced to eat or give Sunbeam a ride to search for me in a forest of dead trees. Father got him for us to ride when we were younger, and he was a very fine horse. I loved him. And he loved me.

Then I saw Sunbeam riding Whitewing, her brows widened into a tragic crease across her forehead. "Gilda! Gilda!" she screamed. "It's all my fault, Gilda," she called, riding and riding, only stopping to wring her head in her hands. Tears rained down her face.

I looked upon my beloved, and my heart broke for her brokenness because we were both doomed together: me chained in a cave while she ran free yet captive by her sadness in the outside world.

"Sunbeam! It's not over! The game isn't over. I'm here!" I shouted.

"Gilda! I'm lost without you," she cried. "Gilda, I'm so sorry," tears streamed and streamed down her cheeks.

And then suddenly, the cloud of the vision started to fade, along with Sunbeam's voice as she called out "Gilda! Gildaaaa! Gildaaaaa!" until it all merged into one distant echo—fading away—and the cloud of the vision began collapsing under a big, black-hearted silhouette—slowly breaking in two—but still as one.

"Here Sunbeam. I'm here." I muttered in a pool of sweat. And for many seconds, I lay swooning until I whispered once more, "Sunbeam?" but heard nothing, except silence in Wolford's cave. The vision had left as quickly as it came. But I sensed whatever this ability was . . . this seeing, I would have to nurture it. It was my only way to get out of that hole.

I feared if I stopped seeing her, I might forget her, and she'd die to me, like my hopes dying in that dungeon. And our oneness of heart, mutually doomed, would crack—completely in two.

All I could do was curl up in my captor's cave, my head against the excess heap of coiled chains. I sobbed and sobbed and sobbed.

I only knew that I wanted to do it again. I wanted to see beyond the pit because in that vision, the darkness bowed down to me. I wanted to see Sunbeam and all the life outside while I was still chained inside. Yes, I wanted freedom. I wanted the truth.

Now at this point, as I lay recounting all the things I'd seen and heard, my senses were sharper than ever—and very, very suddenly—out of nowhere—SNAP!—a terrible noise disrupted my thoughts. My senses already acute—I sprang up—and listened, barely breathing, and kept completely still. And for what seemed like hours, I did not move a muscle and heard nothing for quite some time, until a low groan—a groan of deep grief—resounded in the cave. And before I knew from where it came, I heard quiet footsteps—secretly, cautiously stepping, and I turned my head in all directions to hopefully find that it was only a rodent, or some sediment falling from a rock. And in that moment, along with the recent sequence of bewitching events, my mind was overcome with dread. So, I tried to block out the noise and acted as if it were nothing and closed my eyes. But then, the steps moved closer, more slowly—very, very slowly, as if whoever it was tried not to disturb or wake me. Quietly closer, carefully—crept the hushed footsteps, with deliberate intent. *Oh, it's only a rat crossing the cave, or the runoff dripping down the rock,* I told myself, trying to contain my restless terror.

Then, the footsteps stopped. And everything went silent. All I heard was husky breathing from somewhere in the cave, and I knew by the sound of the breathing, it was *not* the one I hate. Now at this point, my pulse pounded rapidly, and I lay, enveloped in sheer terror, until I burst out, "Who's there?"

I listened, waited. My heart raced. Who, or what, was creeping through the pit?

And in a flash, a figure passed! I caught a brief glimpse of it in the flicker of its lantern—and in the suddenness of the situation and in complete shock . . . down in that dungeon, to my horror . . . to my utter confusion—yes, I'm sure of it—I had just seen—my FATHER!

CHAPTER TWELVE

PRESENT
13 YEARS OLD

Holding cell, Realm of the Dark Night

The memory fades away. The witchy, green glow pulses like one last heartbeat. I spring up, gasping for breath, dizzy and clammy until—thump-thump—the green glow flashes and collapses all in one beat. The light of the crystal is gone.

I lie in my cell, trying to catch my breath, my muscles like putty as I come out of the haze. I wake from that hellish memory, only to open my eyes and exist in a second captivity: a dark, mysterious realm. *Why am I here? It's not fair! And why—my own father? Why was he there?* I look down and find my fist clutching the stone. The crystal is hard and unbreakable in my hand, just like my heart.

Granted, I am no longer in Lord Wolford's dungeon, but he still locks me up in every corner of my mind. *My stone will help me. I will escape.* I'm starting to decode its visions. Each time my crystal thrusts me backward, I sense what deed must be done to go forward.

In a strange way, this dungeon feels worse than Wolford's because I can't astral travel the planes. I haven't figured out exactly why. The last thing I remember is being in Wolford's cave—and Sunbeam had come to the Valley—and Wolford with his terrible claw was trying to gouge out my heart—then BOOM! I wake up in this cell. Where's my silver cord? Surely, I'll find it. Is it still intact?

My powers have never let me down. I will find out who put me here. No, the game isn't over. Not yet.

CHAPTER THIRTEEN

GIL'DA

PAST
YEARS AGO

Valley of Dry Bones

I started perfecting my craft back in Wolford's dungeon. He made me an offer. "It is time, little wolf. Put your powers to use. Catch sinners. Punish evil," he said.

"What do you mean?"

"I shall send you forth to collect debts, child. Scout out sinners who owe me debt for their wrongs. If you bring justice, in turn, I will grant you release."

"What? You'll let me go?" I sat up to listen.

"Yes, but with stipulations. Capture lawbreakers. In exchange for these lawbreakers, you will be granted release to roam the entire underworld—and ethereal realms."

"I don't want any part of your work," I smirked and turned away.

"You want pardon from time in this hole? Be useful, child. Go through Ozmandia and bring outlaws to me," Wolford commanded. "Each sinner given over for their crime is more time you will earn. Your reward shall be recreation in the Valley of Dry Bones—and furlough to roam the celestial spheres."

"Pardon is for prisoners who've done wrong. I've done nothing to deserve this pit."

"Who said life was fair, little girl? Life is gloom and despair. You might as well play dirty, as long as you keep your hands clean. This, too, you shall learn."

"How can I capture anyone when I'm stuck in this hole? I need more!"

"More? I shall gift you with more." He grimaced. "With this gift, you will dance in delight under moons of seductive sorcery."

"You? Give me a gift?" I sneered.

"Oh, child, if you were not such a dunce, you would never ask me that question. A gift comes with a price. The hour has come for a proposal—A PACT." He picked up the *Book of Shadows* in my chamber and opened it. "If you agree to my offer?"

"Well, let's hear it." I wasn't agreeing to just anything, but the thought of free time got my attention.

He swirled his claw—and to my shock—a cloudy mirage appeared in the dungeon: an enchanting illusion that displayed Wolford's high throne; the finest cuts of diamonds and bedazzling gems; tasty delicacies of breads, sparkling cider, and sweets from the wealthiest cities—and his guild of golgums—who all bowed and served him. The mirage beckoned me.

"Marvel! Consider the wonder that magic will achieve, the pleasures it can bring," he boasted. "It will make you vow to study nothing else. Grounded in the secret arts, moon phases and astrology, your insight shall transcend, and you may perform your cunning for yourself. In return, you will be rewarded. But for secret knowledge in these darker mysteries, there comes a price."

"I can perform my own spells. I will make my own sun dawn for me. I don't want anything from you—only out of this hell!" I said.

"I have come from hell to show you how. To show you others' sins. To offer you a chance to bring justice. Little wolf, only wolves defeat wolves. Send these lawbreakers to hell. Examine their faults and dispositions, for their folly will bring you glee. Lock them up and get honor!"

"Give me time to consider . . . I . . . I have questions . . ."

"I have not the time for frivolous questions. Silly girl, the stars move, and the clock will strike. Time will not wait."

"Fine. I will hear more of it."

"Give me your ear. Listen closely." He held up the *Book of Shadows* in front of me. "I, Lord Wolford, hereby stretch my arm and extend the *Book of Shadows* to you. Your sorcery shall capture sinners' souls and bring them to me—to dissolve in the fire, so that you may roam free in the Valley of Dry Bones! And you will be granted honor and power in the underworld, and time to travel in unseen realms and celestial spheres among the stars. You have had time to read the book and only toy in its wizardry. But, the PACT binds you to its black magic and there with it, comes more power. Now, to bind this agreement: Will you sign your name in the book? And will you stamp it with your blood as a seal?" He swirled his claw, and a quill appeared between his long fingers.

My heart pounded. In less than a minute, my thoughts considered a thousand possibilities. But then—why refuse? I'd been in darkness long enough. This furlough would allow me unguarded time from the pit and may help me find Sunbeam. It could help me find the truth! That's all I was seeking—truth and freedom. And although I felt unsure, I had to make my choice.

"I . . . I . . . I consent."

"Sign here, child." My hand trembled as he handed me the quill. He pricked my finger with the sharp tip of it. A drop of blood bubbled red on my fingertip. And I signed my name inside of the book—and stamped it with my own blood. *My God, my God. What have I done?* I thought. *I pictured the man of light's face weeping. Why was I seeing him?* I looked at the ground.

Wolford stepped closer and ran his claw down my cheek. “Now, little wolf, no more talk of this man of light and seeing the sun. It’s for weaklings.” He dropped the *Book of Shadows* on the ground. THUD! Immediately, I saw a small shadow move through the chamber. “Yes, that is it, young wolf. You will see. You will know what to do.” He turned and exited.

Finally, he had gone! I wrung my head in my hands. Again, and without knowing why, I recalled the man who glowed and his words: *This seed grows in darkness but blooms in the sun.* I opened my hand. The tiny scar from that seed he planted in my hand was still there—on the same hand Wolford pricked me. Then I thought of Sunbeam: our times running in the grass with Whitewing, the lavender sunsets and pink candy snaps Father would bring us. With this furlough time, maybe I could still find her—and break out.

I picked up the *Book of Shadows* to begin my magic. I searched the ancient pages, looking for the best spell to arrest these guilty lawbreakers running free back home on my island in Ozmandia. A twinge of guilt pierced me. But then I thought: *Why should criminals run free, while I, an innocent victim, am locked up? Besides, it was in exchange for rewards. They owed debts! At least he wasn’t sending me after innocent souls, but after lawbreakers. So, what did I owe these vigilantes?*

Instantly, what came next startled me. The same shadow from a moment ago passed once more through the chamber. I looked right, then left—and—”Sssss!”—I heard a hissing sound.

“Show yourself!” I said.

The shadow zipped to the ground. I looked down at my foot, and my eyes fell on a snake! “Shoo! Shoo!” I kicked. But it wouldn’t go. It slithered against my foot and coiled into a circle, staring at me, frightened. Strangely, when I looked closer at its face, I felt sorry for it. For when I looked into its beady eyes, I saw confusion, and I felt immediately connected to it. And with the *Book of Shadows* in my hand, it struck me that this snake and I might have a magical connection. I sensed this creature could teach me wild and wondrous things. It stared with lost, black round eyes, as if it knew me, like a stray animal needing a home.

I felt it was safe, so I picked it up. It coiled around my hands and up my arm as if hugging me. I thought of Sunbeam and how we'd catch animals in the cypress trees and play with them: ferrets, birds, squirrels, and even snakes. Sunbeam was leery of the diamond backs, but I wasn't. They slithered to me, never striking, and I would pick them up, pet their scales, and feed them. "How strange, I managed to find you here," I said and petted it.

"No sssss-illy. You didn't find me. I found you."

What on earth? Am I dreaming? "Y . . . y . . . you can talk? I must be dreaming! What is this place where animals speak?" I pinched my face to make sure I was awake. I looked at the *Book of Shadows*. "Oh! How wonderfully bewitching!"

"Yes, and like you, I live among darkness and hidden rocks. I'll never leave you alone," said the snake.

"How did you find me?" I raised an eyebrow, skeptical.

"I'm your familiar," it hissed.

"My what?"

"Your familiar! A friend. I have peeped. I have listened. I understand your gloom and am here to comfort you. We are familiar."

I flipped through the book, making sure this wasn't some mean trick the bony golgums had played. I searched the contents. "Let's see . . . familiar . . . shadow . . . familiar . . . here it is!" I traced my finger under the line and read it aloud:

"A familiar is a gift,
but comes with a price,
a shapeshifter in spells,
so feed it well,

and treat it nice."

I continued reading aloud: "It also reads here, 'give your *familiar* a name it best serves.'"

"Well? What are you going to name me? And what can I get you? There must be something you desire?" Its black eyes gleamed.

"Oh, what should I name you?" I held up my snake. I thought about the many possible names, and it curled around my neck.

An icy heat went through me. Wolford wanted me to capture lawbreakers? I saw a flash of me catching the biggest lawbreaker of all: Wolford! If anyone owed a debt, it was him—for not playing fair.

"Vengeance!" I said. "Your name will be Vengeance, but Vengy for short." I smiled. Vengy slithered around my neck. I petted him. Although he couldn't smile back because he was a snake, we understood each other, as if we spoke the same language. He looked at me with his black eyes, eager to please, ready to carry out anything I ordered. "I can be and do anything you desire. I shape-shift. I dance. But most of all, I peep. I listen and whisper all the things that trouble you. We are familiar," he said.

Then what came next was unfathomable.

"OW!" I yelled. A sharp ache stabbed my eyes.

"Oh misssss, what is wrong?"

"My eyes! My eyes are burning!" My eyes started to burn hotter than before, but then cooled, and everything became crisp and clear. They glowed their sharp, green beams against the wall. And my mind electrified in a new way. Before I knew it, I was downloading Vengy's thoughts into pictures! And I could see through my familiar's eyes! Oh, how magnificently bewitching!

"Can you ssssss—eeee?" he hissed.

"Yes. How wonderful! A metaphysical magician! Seeing through the eyes of a snake! Is this not what everyone desires?

To see all things that move between the quiet poles and alleys? To see into hidden rooms and tables where much wealth is at stake? Oh, I can see. This is a world that will bring much profit and delight!

"Vengy, you will go and be my eyes—and I will see beyond this pit. And you will bring back all sinners to me. You will listen and obey. Between you and me, I'll get rewards, and Wolford will cut me free."

"Oh misssss! Yesssss! I am your familiar! You can sssseeeeee!"

Vengy coiled his black and green scales into a S-shape, swaying charmingly with his tail on the ground and his head high in the air. "Sssseeeee miss! I can stretch my reptilian scales as far as the mind of mankind will allow."

We laughed. And we danced down in the devil's hole. But Vengy's laugh sounded like a slew of hisses. "Oh Vengeance, you will help me get free," I said. "And how will we plan these divinations of escape? Very carefully. And how will revenge feel? Delicious."

Then out of nowhere, I felt a sharp sting. I looked down to find my finger was bleeding.

"Ow! You bit me!" I snapped at Vengy. Two fang holes were on my skin where Wolford marked me with the quill. "Why'd you do that?" I slung the snake down.

"Oh misssss! I'm ssss-orry. So ssss-oooryy. You said the word *delicious*. And I am hungry. Do you have something to eat? Do you promise to feed me and keep me alive?"

"Yes, you will be fed. But don't ever bite me again, Vengeance!" I warned.

CHAPTER FOURTEEN

PRESENT
13 YEARS OLD

Holding cell, Realm of the Dark Night

I wake up. *Oh, poor Vengy.* A tear slides down my cheek.

You see, after nine months in this new cell, my cause is still to soak in the bliss of vengeance. Why? I'm still stuck. Despite Wolford not being here physically, I keep seeing that devil in the corner of my cell, with his claw, hearing his voice coax me onward. "Come with me, child," he would say. "Together, we shall defy your silly fantasies about seeing the sun. I know your gift, you are the One Called, and in time, I will give you full power with me, your prince, Lord Wolford, if you continue in the work."

You see, I thought I'd reached the extent of my powers, but I'm starting to think this serpentine stone adds a new dimension. It's a dimension that I never want Wolford to know—ever—because it takes me back, makes me remember all the things I forgot under the stupor of my drug. And in each of these nightmares the stone summons, I grow as hard as this stone. I believe it's building me up for something greater . . . maybe more evil I must capture. Justice! Blood! And each time the crystal casts its witchy haze, every flicker ignites a rage within me that kindles in this dark space.

Suddenly, as I awaken further, I start to sweat. I reach for my elixir. Hadn't he thought to bring me more? Dumb doorman. "Abaddon!" I yell. "Abaddon!"

CHAPTER FIFTEEN

LORD WOLFORD

PRESENT

My Dear Abaddon,

I note with some concern, to the degree of suspicion, at what keeps our enemy from putting an end to our mental attacks. However, do not yield. Use your mastery to incite misdirection.

Gilda continues in a weakened state. Ones like her are easier to regain, for the injuries have already been done. It is rare that girls like her make it out of the darkness, once taken captive by it. Remember, easier are the ones who suffer unjustly, than the ones who suffer justly. This unjust injury keeps the victim bound, for they've done nothing to deserve the blows of it. Marvel at this matter! They rarely find joy or understanding.

Be watchful, though. Gilda is shrewd and powerful. Yet, she can be enticed to abandon herself without restraint to her wilder passions. Keep on, it is inevitable that she will feel the flames of disorderly desire fiercely within her heart. In fact, so much so, that if you withhold her drug, she can be reduced to a wild mare, stomping at the ground and shivering.

So, I tell you, her good sense will pale when her body is drowning in lusts. And this illness will make her almost unrecognizable, to others and even unto herself. It can do a great deal of harm to the soul.

A feminine gender, her small mind can be enticed to foolishness and petty matters. Stir her desires for what haunts most of these females: imaginary men who are, one, like some thunderous, patriarchal figure who will always protect her, and two, that physical type. One that makes her feel good and evil altogether, that thrill in the chase they are usually after: some cruel, unreachable god that arouses secret obsessions, and will have her faint and swooning. She, being gullible and misguided, will call it 'love.'

I have sent a regiment to spy on what keeps Him, who brings the sun, from the door of her realm. If He tarries too long, I proclaim victory. But dear Abaddon, stay aware! He could come soon. And once he does, we both know—whatever door he opens, no one can shut, and what he shuts, no one can open. Do not delay.

Your Prince,

LORD WOLFORD

CHAPTER SIXTEEN

PRESENT
13 YEARS OLD

Holding cell, Realm of the Dark Night

I'm going to die if he doesn't bring my elixir. "Abaddon! ABADDON!" I've been screaming for what seems to be hours. I'm dizzy. Everything's a blur.

Once again, since that first sip Abaddon brought me, I'm back at step one: a slave to the drink I hate, but it's justified. I love the rush of it. Why refuse what I enjoy? I deserve it. Besides, I'll only take one more dose, then I'll put it down. I won't pick up again until I sort out my plans.

Drink this courage, child, it dulls weakness and sharpens powers.

See, Wolford gave me the elixir when I needed to do hard things. It wasn't easy catching lawbreakers. Things got dirty. After all those years in the underworld, I realized I could cope when I took it. Besides, it's not my fault I got on it. I don't regret it. It makes a gloomy heart tolerable.

Where is this new doorman? A-bad—or whatever his name, hasn't returned.

My muscles begin to tighten. I'll be convulsing soon. In sheer desperation, lost in the dark, I mutter, "God, if you're out there, give me strength."

In the very next second, I feel a breeze on my face. Then something touches the back of my shoulder and glides across my back like warm springtime. I sit up. Instantly, I feel a warm tingle on the palm of my hand—right on the place the tiny seed scarred me as a child. My eyes begin to burn. And I can't believe what they see: a green leaf. Right here, in the most barren, rocky place with no life or water. The greenest leaf I've ever seen is growing up through some tiny crack in the concrete. And although it's a mere sprout, it's the greenest, brightest color my eyes have ever beheld. Even greener than my stone! And a different hue of green: bright, like springtime. Upon seeing it, a ray of sunshine warmth washes over my chest. *Is this another vision? If it is a dream, I can sense reality in it.*

Instinctively and without knowing why, achy from drug withdrawal, I crawl to the greenness growing through the tiny fissure: the only sign of life I've seen in years. I gaze at it. Surprisingly, peace begins to calm my senses. And the more I stare at this small sprout, the more it soothes my mind. Entranced, I spot something peculiar on the sprout, small, but arresting my full attention. Looking for a sign, I glance at my trusty stone dangling on my chest for an answer—but nothing. No signs. So, I lean in and get a closer look at this leaf. *Am I seeing things?* For the white veins of the leaf display what looks to be a word, like intricate, woven calligraphy by a skilled craftsman. Cautious, I touch the leaf. It's soft like silk. I squint to read the veins on the leaf. The words spell:

Εγώ είμαι

How strange. It's written in some other language. Mesmerized, I study this mystical leaf. *Wha . . . ?* I try to sound out the mysterious words.

BAM! BAM! BAM! In a second, this moment is broken by a harsh pounding at my door.

"Miss Gilda? Miss Gilda, let me in."

It's him, the doorman, A-bad . . . Abaddon? Whatever his name is.

"Go away!" I say. I toy with the leaf, captivated. As I examine it—out of nowhere—the tiny seed-scar on the palm of my hand pulses gold and shimmers—then is gone. *What in the name of . . . ?*

"Miss Gilda! It's urgent you open the door!"

"Not now! Go away!" All I can do is admire the leaf and bask in its spring. Everything around me is hazy and muted except for the leaf, and the feeling of a colorful dream. I recall blue skies, green trees, and flocks of birds: memories of Sunbeam and I rising at dawn to run outside and ride Whitewing in the yellow sunrise. It's as if the leaf sparks colorful thoughts. *Gilda, we'll always go together,* I recall Sunbeam's words. *Her green eyes sparkled in the rays. We laughed. We always laughed.*

"Miss Gilda? What's going on in there?"

"Not now!"

"But your elixir, Miss Gilda. Open the door!" He screams. "You need your drug!"

Who needs drugs at a time like this? I think.

"Miss Gilda! Gilda! GILDA LET ME IN!" BAM! BAM! BAM!

Pulled away by his hounding, I start to turn away from this little leaf, this new growth. The colorful dream starts to vanish. After I turn around, I see my cell door. I find I'm sweating and in severe pain from withdrawal. I crawl to the door. His voice booms in my cell—*elixir elixir elixir*—causing my craving to rush through me like a tidal wave.

"Miss Gilda! Let me in!"

"I don't have the key! You do! You know I'm locked up!" I'm still crawling to the door.

"Well, I never enter without your consent."

"My drugs! Yes! Open the damn door!" I pant.

In a flash, he opens the cell. I collapse at his feet. "Oh, Miss Gilda, you're in a terrible condition." Standing at the threshold, he holds the cup over the doorsill and tips it toward my lips. I drink and drink and drink. Instantly, the heat and ice pulsate through every vein and muscle, relaxing me. I fall back into a warm blanket of bliss. "Where were you? I've been calling you for hours."

"Oh, Miss Gilda, I do apologize. I returned last night, but assumed you were sleeping."

"You should have knocked."

"I didn't want to wake you."

"Well, by the time you decided to come back around, I could've been dead."

"Oh miss, I am sorry. But let's not be melodramatic," he teases. "I am here now."

Melodramatic? Did he just call me . . . "Well, let's try not to be condescending, will you?"

"Condescending? I only meant that—"

"I know what you meant."

"Well, I'm here, aren't I? Don't be alarmed."

Easy for him. He's not locked in a cell depending on a drug to breathe with no escape. "Don't be alarmed? Wait. What? What are we doing? And why am I here?"

"Miss Gilda, look, I'm only following orders."

"Orders? From whom?"

"I haven't enough knowledge to say. I only know this is some kind of test. I know as much as you—and that's not much."

"OK. As if I haven't had enough games." *As if Sunbeam hasn't played the worst one. Does she ever think of me? Will she return? Our game isn't over yet, and here he is babbling on . . .*

"Miss Gilda, look, try to calm down. Use your time productively."

I clench my jaw and clutch my stone. "Productively? I'm stuck in some hellhole with not a friend in the world. And now you—in here—smug with contempt!"

He doesn't know who I am, or the powers I hold, and what I can do to him. And even more, why have I let him upset me? Arguing with some petty doorman. I decide to stay quiet. He stays casual, standing tall, arrogantly.

Long silence.

"I'm your friend. We are familiar. I, too, know what it's like to live in darkness—forgotten. Do you want me to stay with you?" he asks.

"For what?"

"Well, I only thought that you . . . you . . ."

"That I what?"

"That you . . ." He pauses. "You . . . you're right. I should go."

"What for?" I say.

"I'm under the impression you want me to leave. And I think you're right. I should." Aloof, he turns to leave. His face is flat and indifferent, as if unmoved at all.

"Get out!" I blurt. *Why am I angry? I do want him to leave. Why does he feel familiar?*

"Never hesitate to ask for what you want," he says. "It's my pleasure—and I would like nothing more right now—than to honor your request—and leave." With that, he winks at me, turns, and walks away, calm and cool, and swelling with the fullest of bravado.

CHAPTER SEVENTEEN

GILDA

PAST
YEARS AGO

Valley of Dry Bones

"Your elixir, madam." Vengy raised his snake tail with my elixir coiled inside of it. I grabbed the cup and took a large gulp. "Ahhh! Vengy, how many more sinners must I send to hell?"

"A job that brings you glee," hissed Vengy. "You're exceptionally good at it, madam. The bessst in the valley."

"But at what cost? I'm sick of working for Wolford."

"Well, madam, you do get furlough for it—and delicious dinners instead of slop. And look at your black diamond from Lord Wolford. Sssstunning!" His black eyes gleamed. "And, you keep me well fed."

"That I do, Vengeance."

"Sssspeaking of food . . . I'm hungry," he hissed.

"You're always hungry."

Vengy's beady snake eyes narrowed on my finger. "No, Vengy! Don't even think about it! You will wait. We're about to catch one." I walked to my table of secret arts, which held various potions, stones, and other things a sorceress would have on hand. "Hmm. Let's see what we'll use here. Moonstone? No. Toad leg? Not quite. A Tiger's Eye? Yes. This one's right!"

I threw down the tiger's eye, a glorious stone in gemology. My eyes began to burn, then glowed green, lighting the chamber.

"Dear Tiger's Eye,
Golden, red, and brown,
Cast forth your hunter's sight,
Throughout my town."

A hazy fog appeared as a mirage. I stared into the live scene: a group of townspeople having ale at their local pub in Ozmandia. Despite my captivity far away, hidden deep down in the Valley of Dry Bones, I had fostered my supernatural sight to see towns and all the goings-on. I searched out lawbreakers for Wolford—whom I hated. In exchange, I got things I wanted: jewels, furlough, good food instead of slush, and respect in the valley.

"OK, let's see who we have here. Hmm. That one looks promising." The sorcerous haze showed a man of about thirty years old in torn clothes and a painful hunger for riches. "That derelict looks like an easy target. What's his background, Vengy? Bring me his record sheet."

"What number is he, madam?"

"Number 669537896."

"To hear is to obey. Here is your lissssst, madam." Vengy handed me the man's offense sheet.

"Let's see here." I read his record aloud. "Thievery. Money. Money and thievery. Envy. Jealousy. GUILTY! Are you ready, Vengy?"

"Ready to serve, madam. I'm your familiar."

"Stay back." I began my incantation:

"As good moors obey their lords,
Take my eyes upon thee,
My familiar, through you, I will see.

"Go where I send,
Shapeshift into sin,
That seduces the thief,
He thinks he can win?

"Go, hunt! Through you, I see,
and bring back swiftly,
The guilty treasury!"

In a flash, Vengy began to shapeshift. "That's it, go! Gooo! Catch the damn crook!" And as he slithered out, my eyes burned hot as fire—and in a flash—Vengy transported, shifting into the shape of a silver coin. And he dropped into the pocket of a town judge. I downloaded Vengy's thoughts, saw and controlled the whole scene in my mirage:

At the local pub, Vengy, as a silver coin, poked slightly out of the local judge's pocket. The judge had his share in ale, chattering with boozy, red cheeks and a big nose. The talent shined and gleamed, and as expected, caught the eye of the thief—who studied it for many minutes, and was seduced by its sheen. The thief slid closer to the judge. The judge, being tolerant, smiled.

"How go it now, Lad?" said the judge. "I pardoned you in court today. Come, sit beside me! Have a drink, being that you are freed!"

"Yes, dear Judge. You showed me mercy. And for that, I will never steal again!" But, overcome by his vice, the crook quietly slipped his fingers into the judge's pocket, not knowing it was a biting serpent. And when that swindler lay hold of the judge's shiny coin—a bite!—OUCH!—then a sting—and everything went black. He woke up in my lair—never to go back.

The thief, cuffed in iron, awoke. "What? Where am I? Who are you?"

The thief held tightly to the silver coin, which to his great shock, transformed into my loyal snake, Vengeance, and slipped through his fingers.

"Oh! A snake?" He flinched. "Is this a joke? Surely, a magic trick!" he said in a trembling voice.

"No joke at all, sir. You, number 669537896, are hereby charged with theft from the judge's pocket. Do you plead guilty to stealing the judge's money? And to your sin?"

"Number what? I have a name! Where am I? How did I get here?"

"This is my last time asking you the same question: Do you plead guilty to the crime of theft from the judge's pocket?"

"No . . . I . . . What is this? What is going on? I planned to return it."

"If you say you have no sin, you deceive yourself! For that, you'll be turned over to death."

"Death? You are mad! What theory is this? Let me go! Please!"

"Guilty, sir."

"I didn't mean any harm! I took it to feed my children who are sick with hunger," he pled.

I scanned his written record. "It reads here, you have no children. Now, you dare tell a lie? This lie, too, will be added to your list of sins."

"You are mad! I demand a fair trial!"

"You had your chance to play fair. GUILTY! Hurry, Vengy. For soon, I turn this thief over to the devil."

Vengy slithered to number 669537896.

"Oh, I'm sssss-ooo hungry!" hissed Vengy, staring at the thief.

"Your food! Take just what you need to fill your hunger. Keep him alive," I said.

Vengy's mouth stretched back a mile wide, baring two sharp teeth, ready to strike.

"No! PLEASE NOOO!" begged the thief. "I can pay it back! NOOO!" He flailed on the ground.

I turned away. I took a big drink of elixir, trying to drown out the screams. Then I heard the hiss and—STRIKE—as my familiar sunk its fangs into the thief's flesh, sucking his blood.

"Just enough to get full, Vengy. Then I'm turning him over to Wolford." I had my back turned to the bloody scene, gulping my drug.

After a few moments, and more pleading the thief went completely silent. I turned back to face the dreadful scene, to find the offender's face drained of all color. And Vengy, showing no signs of stopping his feeding, I ordered, "Enough! Vengy, enough!"

With a loud suckle, my snake pulled its fangs out of the thief's vein. And dripping with the fresh blood of a sinner, hissed, "Oh! There is nothing sweeter than vengeance!"

Hours had passed since the thief had gone. Another one brought down, adding to the many numbers. I stared at the ceiling, trying to sleep. Vengy slid up next to me with my elixir. "They are just numbers, missss," he comforted. "Lawbreakersssss!"

"Yes. To that devil everyone is faceless, Vengy. Just another number added to his guild. Men, women, children. No matter. I'm starting to think that maybe justice doesn't mean someone gets locked up. Maybe it just means someone, anyone, pays the price for the wrong."

In the next moment, there was a knock on my chamber. "Madam, may we enter?" It was a golgum.

"You may."

The golgum opened the door. He grabbed a hooded troublemaker by the neck and threw him into my chamber. He had a sack over his head, a spit hood to keep him from biting. So, his face was concealed.

"Madam, here's number 277181958. He is one of our very own, a golgum, but not obeying—and asking too many questions. Keep watch on him until we can get him into a cage."

"Treacherous hounds! I've done no wrong!" said the hooded man, "I have a right to—"

"Have right to what? You have no rights here!" The golgum punched the hooded man in the face.

"Wait! What has this man done?" I interrupted. "Why are you throwing him in *my* chamber?"

"This nuisance wants to creep around the pit and your chamber to spy. Well, he can sit here till he's sick of it!" Then he turned to the masked derelict and pointed his long finger at him. "This is your last chance. If we catch you prowling around the madam's chamber again, we are taking you to the master for a flogging!" They stormed out.

The hooded golgum sat up and shook the dirt from his cloak. Despite the disrespect he'd just taken, there was a dignity about him.

Long silence.

"Who are you? What's your number again?" I asked.

"I am number 277181958." He raised his shoulders.

"Is it true? Were you snooping around my quarters?"

"I'm afraid you're a she-devil!" he said. "The guild knows of your power."

"Oh? do I have horns and clubbed feet?" I smirked. "What, sir, do you want with me?"

"I am not at liberty to answer that now."

"I sense something different about you. Why are you with the guild?"

"Rewards."

"Rewards?" I asked.

"Yes. The same rewards you, too, earn from Wolford. I studied many books, acquired much knowledge in philosophy, physics, and law. 'First-rate intelligence!' Wolford would boast about me. He gave me an offer. So, I agreed to use my intelligence for the guild in exchange for finer things I could provide my family. But things did not go as planned. As for you, I have seen and watched. The only difference between us is that you work for him due to unfortunate circumstances, mine, due to choices. But the end result will be the same."

"How dare you put me in your category. You don't know me!"

"I know enough to see you are full of pride. As I was, long ago," he said. "You are just like me when I was young."

"Me? Like you? You are brazen, sir! You think I have a choice other than to do that devil's work?"

"Yes, I do. You always have a choice." His eyes narrowed on the black diamond around my finger. "I have been in hell long enough to realize those rewards will not fill your heart."

"What do you know? You think you're some kind of teacher?"

"That, I am. I will teach you, if you'll listen. When I first laid eyes on you in the Valley, something sparked inside of me. I do not yet have the answer to this question. But forgive me for such boldness, miss—I feel I must protect you."

"Why would a soulless golgum like you want to protect me?" Without knowing why, he reminded me of someone I used to know. *He is a golgum, so it couldn't be possible,* I thought. I recalled the night I saw my father's face pass by the pit. But later, I had dismissed it.

"You can do better," he ordered. "Stop doing the devil's work."

"It's my only chance out of here," I said.

"Listen to me. It will dig a deeper hole."

"Why do you want to help me?"

"I . . . I do not know. But your face reminded me of a person I used to know—long ago."

"You have seen my face, sir. Let me see yours. Please, take off your mask."

In the next second, a rumbling of feet clamored down the corridor and into my chamber. A few golgums barged in holding iron cuffs. "Madam! We found a secure cage for this troublemaker!" One of the golgums held up the chains and turned to number 277181958. "This is the reward for those who creep and ask questions! Who question the master's rules!" Then he punched the hooded man in the stomach, cuffed his wrists, and dragged him out.

CHAPTER EIGHTEEN

PRESENT
13 YEARS OLD

Holding cell, Realm of the Dark Night

It's been hours since Abaddon left. Since then, I've returned to this new leaf growing up through the cement, studying its veins that twist and curl into those strange words that spell:

Εγώ είμαι

What on earth? My stone has remained silent. No signs. I'm drawn to this little leaf. That sense of peace washes over me as I study it, feel it in my hand. *How bizarre . . .*

In the next moment, I hear footsteps in the corridor outside. My thoughts return to Abaddon. *Is it him? I want it to be him. Why? I want him gone.*

"Miss Gilda?" He knocks gently.

"What do you want?"

"I thought you might need more . . . elixir."

"Fine."

"May I come in?"

"I suppose, since your persistence is such a polite way of being annoying."

The door widens, his candle illuminates through the slither of open door, that odd candle he holds, flickering a blue flame. In the other hand, he holds more elixir. He stops abruptly at the doorsill. "Look, Miss Gilda, I wanted to—" He swallows a rock of pride. "I wanted to bring you this. I am . . . sorry for earlier." He stands with his chin raised, aloof, and visibly pushing through this apology. I assume he doesn't apologize often. His eyes look black and brooding.

I get up and move toward the doorsill, wanting the elixir. He hands me the cup. I drink, and this extra dose transports me into a cloud of complete euphoria. It flows through me, lifting my mood into a state of lighthearted jest. "Well, you've been a bad—a bad-baddon," I wink.

"It's Abaddon, miss." He chuckles. "And . . . had I known that you . . ."

"That I what?"

"Your condition." He starts to move toward me, but stops, careful not to step too close.

I'm now lying on my back, intoxicated in my cloud of complete comfort. His feet remain planted. I notice him studying me. *Why is he here? Why so kind? The other doorman never . . . and those smoldering eyes . . . if I could see what's swirling in those two black orbs.*

"I'd feel terrible leaving you like this," he says.

"Oh, I'm fine."

"Well, I could stay for a bit, if . . . if that is OK . . . it must get lonesome in here."

"I told you. I'm fine."

Silence.

"I'd like nothing more than to have a chat," he says.

"Well, since you're so riled up about it . . . I guess you can," I say. There is something familiar about him.

"Are you sure, Miss Gilda? I don't want to intrude."

"Intrude?" I look around my empty cell. "What's there to intrude on?" *Why am I letting him in here?* I think to myself. *And after he acted so arrogantly!*

"Sure, Miss Gilda. My pleasure," he says. Before stepping closer, he scans the cell as if looking for some enemy. Apprehensively, he takes a seat on the floor of my cell. Still lying down, I raise my head and lie on my side, arm tucked behind my head to face him. Looking up at him, his back rests against the iron wall. He wears a black shirt. The collar is cut into a loose V-neck, which highlights the top of his athletic chest and smooth skin. I catch his dark eyes reflecting the blue flame of that candle he carries. He sets it down. It flickers dimly in the dark cell.

"That flame. So blue," I say.

"Well, blue is the warmest color," he says.

"Or, like I said before—the coldest," I smirk. *Just like my heart.*

He swallows hard and looks at me, as if he's found some lost treasure. Then our eyes meet, and he holds his gaze for a quick moment, like he's studying a valuable diamond. I turn away. "That crystal, on your chest" he says, "it's intriguing."

"It's a stone. Green serpentine," I reply. "It's the hardest stone to break."

In the next moment, he reaches down like he's going to grab it. "May I?" he asks.

"Be careful with it," I reply.

His hands roll over the stone's texture. "It's so smooth." His voice suddenly becomes velvety, almost spellbinding. "But you're right" he says, "very hard to break." As his fingers search the stone, dangling on my chest, he seems distracted and lost in thought.

"Yes, very hard to break," I say and take my crystal from him. Just then, I notice a mark on his chest, slightly above his V-neck. It looks like a scar, as if he'd been scratched by some vicious animal—and next to it, some words written in ink.

A claw mark. Wolford? No! Why would I even think . . . stop Gilda! You're imagining things.

"What's that?" I ask.

"Oh, just a marking. It covers a birthmark. I'm not who I am by birth. So, I covered it."

"What's that mean? Who were . . . who are you?"

"It's a long story."

"How old are you?"

He flashes a wide grin. "Well, let's just say I am classic compared to you. I have a timeless look, but strangely, I've never felt more present with anyone as I do right now." He reaches down and touches the ends of my hair, hanging over my torn blouse. "Your hair. It's so black." He notices the tangles. "How long have they kept you in here?"

"Too long," I sigh. "It's going on nine months."

"I can find a basin. I can wash it, if you like."

Looking at him, I try to use my ability to sense his motives. *Why all this concern? Why me?* But his eyes are dark and mysteriously deep. So dark they look bottomless. So deep, like I could fall to my death inside of them. I cannot read anything, not yet. But I feel a strong connection with him. In the next moment, he takes my hand.

"Your hands, and your nails," he says. "Let me get something to clean them."

In an instant, strangely, and before I can even think, my heart is racing, and I can't tell if it's him or the elixir that's making it race.

"I have more elixir if you like, Miss Gilda?" he asks affectionately. And before I know it, he's moving closer toward me. He smells like a mix of sweet jasmine and leather. "Gilda, come here," he says. "Open your mouth." He holds the cup to my lips, and I drink. "Gilda, you're trembling," he says and pulls me toward him, concerned.

In the next moment, everything seems to stop, and in sheer elation of the drink, with his arms around me and wrought with exhaustion, I collapse onto his chest. And a new kind of warmness flows through my body. And what comes next, I can't even believe. He strokes my hair. "Are you OK?" he asks. And before I even know what's taking place—strange things are happening. His hands find my neck and his fingers glide down my arms. And I'm leaned back, my hair splayed out all over his chest, closer than ever, next to the strange marking inked on his skin that reads:

καταστρέφω

"I understand how you feel. I, too, have lived among darkness," he says.

All I can do is fall into the bliss of the elixir and his supporting presence—and wondering how—within seconds, he's so close I can feel his warm breath on my neck. And even more—why a strong overflow of emotion is surging through me like a thousand butterflies.

"You . . . you should go," I mutter. I sit up. It's hard to tear myself away.

"Oh! Yes, I should."

I look at the ground. And suddenly, I catch a glimpse of that green plant growing up through the nook of my cell. *What on earth?*

"Yes, Miss Gilda. Goodnight."

"Umm, wait. Can you leave more elixir?" I ask.

"Of course," he says. Then he hurries to leave and hands me the chalice. And as he exits my door, I realize I've let someone inside . . . someone that feels so familiar, a connection I've never felt before.

CHAPTER NINETEEN

LORD WOLFORD

PRESENT

My Dear Abaddon,

Gilda is easier to manage than I presumed. Her abominations cloud her vision. She will pay for these blunders. Keep turning her focus from herself and steer her state of mind to confusion—and her soul to anguish. Also, my boy, use your sensitive charms and pitying gestures to evoke these grieving sentiments all the more.

Working in our favor is the elixir. Since the first sip you gave her, she has returned to enjoy the sparkling chalice that goes down smoothly at first, but later, will bite her like a snake.

I still note, with some suspicion, why HE has not come to her rescue. Time is running out. In the chance He does come soon, I am raising our methods of warfare. Double the potency of the elixir—this will suspend her reality—it will disturb her thoughts—and in her state of anger—

paint dark fantasies of revenge. Double it, my dear Abaddon. Double it! So we can bring her home.

Your Prince,

LORD WOLFORD

CHAPTER TWENTY

PRESENT
13 YEARS OLD

Holding cell, Realm of the Dark Night

On this night, I feel unusually cautious about opening the door. It has been one night since Abaddon left. Now here he is, on the other side, knocking.

"Miss Gilda?"

Silence.

Should I let him in? It's quiet and boring in here and . . . and . . . no. In no way am I letting him inside. Ever since last night, never before had I sensed such a connection. The last time I felt that instant friendship was with Vengy, my familiar. But with this doorman, it's a bit different. It's mysterious. It's enthralling. And each time he knocks, I can barely contain a magnetism pulling me toward his velvety voice, his sweet-leathery smell, his smooth, glimmering skin. I mean, he's trying to help me. But I sense danger—caution and adventure all in one rush.

"I have your elixir, miss."

Who would have thought some doorman would become such a nuisance? My priority is to escape this cell. That is the only mission. I do not know the reason for my sudden curiosity with this doorman. And maybe that is the very reason for the draw—because what I come to know, I may like. But what I do not know, I can't be distracted by—right? I think it's best not to know. I remain silent. I only need that elixir!

"Miss Gilda, is everything OK?"

To think here I am, battling to open my door or not, distraught with angst, and he hasn't even one iota of my secret thoughts. I haven't had a friend or anyone to talk to in a long time. I almost chuckle at the absurdity of it.

"OK, miss, I will leave it at your door." He slips the cup through the slot. There is a long pause. I can feel his charm through the wall. Being a seer, I'm sensitive to energy. His allure seeps into my chamber. For a second, and only for company, I fairly toy with the idea of letting him inside to chat, and perhaps he senses it, too, because he stands and waits at the door for many seconds—until—until his footsteps finally fade down the corridor.

Ahhh! I exhale. He's gone! My heart pounds. It thumps so hard my green stone slightly throbs above the lining of my blouse. I'm swirling in a sea of trepidation. Needing to refocus, I start toward the elixir. I can't wait to drink it; that relief will soon transport me out of this hell. I mean, what do they expect me to do all day in here? I walk to get the drink. I'll be walking on air soon.

I drink. My unrestrained passions detach into a simple thought. Yes, I am the master of myself.

What? Wha . . . wait . . . something is wrong . . . what's happening? Something starts to feel different. Very . . . VERY DIFFERENT. *No, wait . . . it's . . . !* I slam back violently on the floor. *Did they change my dose? It's strong . . . too . . . too strong.* I gasp for air, dizzy in the blur of this tonic and swirling in terror of its all-masterful potency. Flat on my back, my limbs go numb. I can't move, helpless under the power of this severe drug.

My stone's eerie green glow starts to spread out like a green horizon. Black shadows flicker on the wall that look like dancing demons. I clutch the stone and wait for a sign. The demons' silhouettes swirl around me on the ceiling. I'm utterly terrified. In the next second, uncontrollable coldness fills my chest. I feel as cold and hard as the stone in my hand, and I begin to quiver in a mix of love and hatred for *her*—for Sunbeam.

I shake violently on the concrete. The black silhouettes grow taller and taller on the ceiling. Their long, clawed fingers curl, and their hands wave as if casting deep sorcery. They circle around and around. "What's happening to me?" I mutter to my stone. "What are you showing me?" I can barely speak, immobilized by the power of this elixir that's so strong I fear the next breath might be my last. No matter how hellish I sense this nightmare will be, the stone's ghostly door to my past is taking me there whether I fight it or not. It will show me. I must remember. I am a seer. I must see into this past dimension so I can unlock my present prison. So, I hold my breath, and . . . and . . . no . . . go away! Gooo! No . . . NOOO! I fall down into the hellish past I long to forget, transcending further into the portal of the green, serpentine stone.

CHAPTER TWENTY-ONE

GIL'DA

PAST
YEARS AGO

Valley of Dry Bones

Days turned into months, and months turned into years in Wolford's cave. Time ticked on. "You know, Vengy. It's strange how time changes things; it can make a terrible place seem normal," I said.

"I'm here with you, missss. I'm not leaving. We are familiar."

Still in Wolford's underworld, I thought of Sunbeam and what she was doing. Was she thinking about me, too? Was she searching for me? Or had she moved on with her life? And dissolving in a shadow of memories, suddenly, my senses heightened into another dimension. I felt like someone was pushing me to the side and entering the cave, as if I were transcending into the beginning of time, some place from long ago. Every part of me became engulfed, and once again, I was swept away from the cave, and into another vision.

I saw Sunbeam and myself. We were riding our horse, Whitewing. He carried us through the greenest fields. Sunbeam rode in the front, with me in the back. Her long blonde hair blew

in my face, and our locks flailed in the breeze into one big golden tussle, until you didn't know whose hair was whose.

"Whitewing! Stop!" Sunbeam shouted in the wind as he sped us through the field. Whitewing, an obedient and good horse, slowed to a stop. Then my beloved Sunbeam dismounted and took me under a large, beautiful tree growing in the field. And she surprised me with colorful candies. We always ate those at the golden hour when the sky was peach and lavender. She held up her half of the heart-shaped, gold locket. "Isn't it the most beautiful thing you've ever seen?" Sunbeam smiled, eyes sparkling in the sun. "We're always going to be close. You will always have the other half." I held up my piece. And in the vision, when I held it, suddenly, my half began to burn my hand. The one she held in her hand shined more golden while mine began to blacken and tarnish like coal. "What's happening, Sunbeam?"

And then my heart started to blacken along with the broken, tarnished locket in my hand. I looked up, and my beloved Sunbeam was no longer close, but far-far away on the other side of the field, holding her half of the locket, shouting, "Gilda! Where are you? Gilda! I'm so sorry! Don't leave me, Gilda. I didn't mean to! I'm trying to find you. GILDA. GILDAAA!"

And as she yelled and yelled, tears rained down her cheeks as quickly as my locket singed to black. And horrified, Sunbeam's face began to vaporize, and her voice faded until it became a distant echo crying out, "Gildaaaa!"

I shouted back, "Sunbeam? Sunbeam!" until my tarnished locket disintegrated into dust through my fingers. "No! SUNBEAAM!"

"GILDA! GILDAAAA!" her voice continued in desperation, until only her green eyes became large in the vision, searching and wide in a tragic stare. "Gilda, I didn't mean to. I'm going to find you Gildaaaa!"

And then the vision of the cloud began to slowly close, and as it closed, the white cloud of the vision morphed into a cracking, charcoal heart. And what was still as one—had slowly and completely—severed in two.

❧ ❧

Still in Wolford's cave, I lay for many minutes in a pool of sweat. Sunbeam's voice echoed over and over in my mind: *Gilda, I didn't mean to. I am going to find you! I didn't mean to. I'm trying to find you!*

I sat up, groggy and achy, and took another sip of the elixir. "Yes, but you caused this. And you haven't! You did this! And you haven't!" I said.

"Missss, are you alright?" Vengy stared at me, eyes gleaming with concern. He slithered close to me.

"Vengy, shouldn't evil be punished? Sunbeam did a wicked thing. She deserves this prison, not me."

"I am hungryyyy, missss. She did commit a crime. We can catch Sunbeam, another number's blood, another lawbreaker," said Vengy.

"I don't know, Vengy, maybe it's not her fault."

"Eye for an eye. Lambs don't defeat wolves. Only wolves defeat wolves," Vengy reminded me. "You don't deserve thissss, misss. I know the feeling of betrayal and confusion. Just because I'm a ssssnake, I know more than you think."

The elixir was numbing my apprehension to inflict justice. *Swing a righteous sword.* I took another drink. And in that moment, I realized that with more of this drug, I could do no wrong, and even more, feel no wrong. All the world was OK. And although I was in hell, it felt like heaven. And oh! You should have felt the freedom I had! To do anything I wanted! And with perfect insight and precision! And all those suggestions from Wolford that once made my stomach churn, all detached and lost meaning. The elixir and *Book of Shadows* opened a gate into some magical place where stars and moon eclipsed into deep mysteries, and all these brilliant fantasies sparkled in a dark sky. Nothing was impossible. I took another gulp of the elixir. And I wondered how I'd ever lived life without it.

Then something else swept over me. As my eyes started to burn hot and glowed green in the chamber, I saw lambs dancing on the stars and leaping over the moon. But in the next moment, the lambs started laughing at me, mocking me, and pointing with a bunch of taunting "Bahahah—bahaha—bahahas!" And their faces looked like all the people who'd ever wronged me. "It's not fair. I'm innocent. Why laugh? I'm innocent!" I said back. But they laughed like annoying sheep in a pasture, with their "bahahah—bahahah—bahahahas!" My stomach winced. I started drifting down from the stars, into some dark oblivion, shouting, "I'm innocent! Innocent! Stop! I'm innocent!"

And suddenly, one of the stars spit fire across the sky and morphed into a wolf—furious—its fangs dripped with blood. It licked its claws. Fire blew from its mouth like a dragon until it sprang and streaked across the sky ferociously and devoured all the sheep that were laughing at my misfortune. And then it perched on the highest star. The star's name was Justice. And the wolf gloated in its glory and roared across the sky so loudly that the whole world heard it, "Do you want to punish evil?"

"Yes! Yes!" Voices of hurt, innocent victims wailed from below. "Punish evil. Punish all evil!"

Yes, the one thing that would set me above all the tormenters and take me higher was that bewitching world of savory revenge, to put to death the babbling sheep that injured me—and this—dare I even think it? This included my dearest lamb of all.

CHAPTER TWENTY-TWO

GIL'DA

PAST
YEARS AGO

Valley of Dry Bones

Still in Wolford's pit, I had just finished counting my crystals, toying with potions for my next hex. My table of magical arts was set.

Vengy poked his head out from a purple potion bottle, filled with scented sticks. He stretched his tail toward me with my drug in the center of his venomous tail. "What can I do? How can I help?" He coiled around the bottle.

I took a huge drink. "Bring more lawbreakers. I want to be released from here. I still cannot find Sunbeam. There seems to be a shield around her. My spells cannot see through it to find her."

"Oh missss! I am hungry!" His black eyes brightened. "What about number 277181958's blood? Can't we find some more chargessss on him?"

"I don't know. He doesn't seem like just another number."

It had been a while since they dragged number 277181958 out. *I must protect you,* he'd said. Now, I didn't trust golgums, but I sensed this one was different. Did he know something? I needed to see his face to read him clearly.

Vengy slithered next to me. "More elixir, missss?"

"Of course, Vengy. You always know. We are familiar." I took a drink. The elixir relaxed me. I plopped down on my bed. A seer's work is never done, another full day of sorcerous potions and manipulating crystals. "Vengy, I'm tired. Bottle up those potions I mixed. And lay the new crystals on the front of the table near the *Book of Shadows*. I will study those later."

"Yes, missssss."

Exhausted, I fell back on my bed and began drifting into slumber. Then silence, stillness—and very weary, my eyelids grew heavy, and I lay completely motionless. I drifted into that place between dreams and consciousness—until something strange overcame my soul. There was an unusual quietness—then a rushing memory awakened: a memory of footsteps. *I know the rhythm of that gait—Father? Am I hearing things?* And for many minutes, I was left motionless—no sound—except the turbulent and sudden beating of my heart. But I dismissed the possibility. *What a ridiculous exaggeration!* Then a resurgence of logic and a rushing of sensible articulation came back to me. *Oh, stop, Gilda. It's not possible. Don't lose your head.*

But as soon as I dismissed those exaggerated thoughts, I heard the footsteps again: they stepped quietly yet with intent. Then came a sigh of deep grief in the cave. "Vengy?" I said. "Did you hear that?" I sat up in the dark.

Vengy slid behind a bottle of potion on the table of secret arts and shapeshifted into a wizard staff. "Vengy?" I looked into the darkness of the cave. And before I knew what was happening, there came a voice:

"Well, youngster, you are grounded in the secret arts, I see!" said the voice.

The voice came upon me so suddenly I didn't know how long it had been there. I sprang up in the blackness and secretly grabbed the dagger I kept next to me when sleeping. I squinted to see in the dark. And there before me, I detected a figure—a spit hood barely outlined in the dark. It was him: number

277181958. He lit a candle in the sconce, then stood, examining my table of sorcery.

"And you are well learned in gemology—all the things strong magic requires," he said. "I have had my eye on you."

I should have been furious with him trespassing into my chamber, but for reasons I couldn't explain, relief washed over me. "You? What do you want here? The guild still has you bound in that hood? You can take off your mask here, sir."

"I am not at liberty to remove my mask. I have only a little time here. I must return before they come back to unlock my cage, only to find it empty."

"You escaped the cage? No one can escape Wolford's bars."

"Escapology, little one! Too much study of science and law is for petty wits. It is black magic that has captivated me. I can escape any trap. Now, come, perform some of your magic." He stood up tall in his long, black cloak.

"Well, I . . . I . . . let's see . . ."

Long silence.

"Well, if you're going to take all night, let me teach you the words of art, rituals, and ceremonies—so that you may conjure up a way out of this hell," he said.

Despite him traipsing in my dungeon, I didn't sense danger. He talked like the instructors did back at school, a firm tone but with intent to push me forward, to help me.

"You are a seer. That, I know," he said. "But you must stop seeing through your snake, Vengeance. You must go into ethereal realms yourself—and fly!"

"How do you know of Vengy? And fly? How?"

"I have been watching you. Astral travel, young one," he said. "And once you have learned, always use it for good. And protect your silver cord. Any sorcerer knows—you must guard your silver cord, so that it's never cut. Or, your soul will be lost, never to return to body."

"Yes, I have read it in the *Book of Shadows*," I said. "I've been working on this divination. I'm seeking truth! I think I have figured a way to astral travel. I am close!"

"Listen, now. Close your eyes and think of where you want to go," he said. "And if you don't know where to go, believe you will be taken to the right dimension. What the mind sees first, the spirit will follow."

I closed my eyes. I took a deep breath. I raised my arms out to the side like wings and began my charms:

"Enchanting hour,
it is I who sees,
cast forth your moonlight,
give me wings!"

Long silence. Nothing.

"Ahhh! I can't do it!" I yelled.

"You can. And you will. Against all odds, believe! It is then you will become strong enough to fly."

"This should do it!" I picked up my red tiger's eye from the table and clutched it in my fist. I closed my eyes again. I took a deep breath and raised my arms like wings:

"Enchanting hour,
it is I who sees,
with the red-eye stone,
give me wings!"

Silence. Nothing.

I threw the tiger's eye against the wall. "Useless!" I sighed.

"Oh, madam. You're all worked up," Vengy slithered next to me, elixir in tail. "Some elixir should help."

Plume looked down at my familiar. "Do not offer what poisons the mind, snake!" he thundered. He took the cup of elixir from Vengy's tail and threw it down. The glass shattered on the ground.

"What are you doing? No!" I blurted. "You had no right!" I bent down to pick up the broken glass and comfort my familiar. "Oh, Vengeance!"

I was on the ground with him.

"Little one, what are you doing down on the ground? Stand up on your feet! There is no time dwelling on what's broken!" he thundered, standing over me with his long cloak.

Vengy raised his head from the dirt and slithered upright into an S. "Oh, I am ssss-orry! I was only trying to help." Vengy shifted his eyes to the black diamond on my finger. "Madam, do you not want more rewards from the master? Do I not get to eat? We have real work to do." Vengy looked at number 277181958. "The master rewards those who catch outlaws, like this one standing here! I am hungry."

"Not now. I will feed you soon."

I turned back to number 277181958. "You know, sir, it's strange, but you remind me of someone," I said. "Maybe you can help me find someone in the guild. I . . . I thought I saw my father . . . his face flashed by one night in the valley. Oh, I know it's a silly thought." I shook my head and looked away.

"Your father?" He stared off in thought. "Youngster, surely, that man cannot be the same man." He put his hand to his chin. His face was still hooded. Deep in thought, he slowly made his way to sit on a nearby rock in the chamber.

In the next second, Vengy slithered speedily and shapeshifted into a thorn on the rock where the masked man was only seconds from taking a seat.

"Vengy, no!"

It was too late. He sat on it. By the time the hooded man realized what happened, Vengy had already morphed back into a snake, hissing away in laughter "SSSSSSS!"

"Cunning little viper! You bit me!" He jumped up as quickly as he sat down.

"Oh, excussssse me, sssssir," Vengy hissed, then slid on the table of arts and shapeshifted into a set of eyeballs, which stared frozen on number 277181958.

"Viper!" snapped the hooded golgum. Then he looked at me. "Onward. Upward!" he warned. "You have no time to play around with snakes."

"You know nothing of Vengeance! And you had no right! He's just here to help! It's my familiar!" I turned away and continued picking up the broken glass of elixir on the ground.

"Do not stay down with it too long, child, or you might end up staying there." And he turned and fled into the night, his long black coattail flowing out behind him.

❧ ☙

A few nights had passed. I couldn't stop thinking about number 277181958. *Why was he trying to help me?* After another day's work for Wolford, I, his "Highest ranking sorceress!" as he'd say, was only human. I had feelings. I got tired. And sometimes, I got blue. Putting the thoughts of the day away, I lay in silence until I began drifting to sleep.

After a while, I was deep in slumber.

Something woke me. Coming to, my eyes focused, and number 277181958 came into view, looming over me. He was wearing the same hood that always covered his face.

"Gilda," he panted. "I had to return!" His heart was pounding so hard I could almost feel it. Then it came over me like a monsoon that this masked man just said my name—my REAL name. How did he know I was Gilda and *not* Sunbeam?

"Gilda?" I questioned him. "Sir, how? HOW DO YOU KNOW MY NAME?" I sprung up for I was still posing as Sunbeam. "Shhh! You must be quiet!" I whispered. My stomach dropped in fear. My hands began to tremble.

"Oh, Gilda." He walked to the sconce and lit a torch. He stood up tall in the firelight in his long, black cloak. Then, he reached his hands toward his face—and—pulled off his mask. I stared at him as if trying to remember him from somewhere, like you would a stranger that you felt you'd seen before. At first, I hardly recognized him, unsure of who he was until I realized—no—yes—surely, it was my own FATHER!—gazing at me with his face contorted and confused.

"Gilda, my daughter," he whispered frantically. "Oh, sweet Gilda, I'm so sorry. I'm your father." Then before I could think, he picked me up in his arms.

"Escapology! I am here to rescue you, my daughter! Be still and hold on!"

He started carrying me out of the cave. "Wait, what is going on?" I said before I could even think. He held me tightly, so I wouldn't fall.

"You must trust me!" In a flash, he was running and running through dark mazes of the cavern—until he'd taken me to the mouth of the cave, which opened into a silvery moonlit night. "We must leave at once!" His breath was heavy and panting, running with me through the silver-lit forest of trees.

"Why? Father, why am I here? Why are you here? What is all this?"

"I'm redeeming what I've done—what I've done to you. The mistake I made," he cried. A tear glinted down his cheek in the moonlight. "I am your father. We are here by different circumstances, but if we do not escape, we both face the same tragic end."

"What have you done? Tell me what's going on!" I pleaded.

But overwrought, and panting for breath as he ran, he wouldn't answer. He just stared ahead, running with me as fast as he could go.

CHAPTER TWENTY-THREE

LORD WOLFORD

PRESENT

My Dear Abaddon,

Well done, my boy! You've rationed enough potency of the drug to excite deterioration, but not enough to kill her. There remains a boundary. We are prohibited from taking her life—for now. Gilda's plan for freedom is altered in the haze of the drug, and her intellect tormented by the abomination of it. The girl troubles herself to gain freedom and truth. In her memories, the exercise of revenge expands through the reflections of her past. Keep doubling the elixir!

Her bewitching powers will be used in our realm once we regain her. She is a powerful force when unleashed. You know this well. Be careful. If she gets suspicious of you, she will destroy you. She is as strong as Sunbeam, but in a different way—fatally viscous. Be watchful.

You know your objective. We will regain Ozmandia! And the people will put out those lamps they burn to our enemy, the God of Lights. This battle is between me and Him—a war of the gods—although we use earthly kings as pawns—and must turn these powerful ones—like Sunbeam and Gilda—to our side.

Sunbeam is out of reach. She has caused me much harm! We will plan an ambush on her at a later time. As for now, Gilda is who we want, who is weakest, and whom we will use to end Sunbeam. These two will crush each other.

Marvel at how these humans destroy themselves. Destroy love! Spill blood! Stomp on peace! Their injured hearts cloud their eyes. They become like the evil under which they've innocently suffered—bitter and unaware of their darkness—which they like to wrap in a bright cloak and call it justice. We need only to place the sword of vengeance in their hands—for indeed—they will slay themselves.

Your Prince,

LORD WOLFORD

GILDA: THE LOST TWIN

CHAPTER TWENTY-FOUR

GILDA

PRESENT
13 YEARS OLD

Holding cell, Realm of the Dark Night

I wake from the past. The light of the crystal fades. *What are you going to do now?* Serpentine asks.

I will escape. And I will become a power the world has never known—a mighty force. No one will even dare think of crossing me again.

The strange weed growing up through the cement catches my eye. *How impossible, this sign of life in this dead place.* It looks bigger, prettier, greener. *How strange.* The veins on the leaf have curled. They beckon me. Those mysterious words that read:

Εγώ είμαι

What on earth? My trusty crystal starts to cast its slime green light. I hold it up. I set my intention. I whisper, "God, if you're out there, give me strength to do the hard thing."

Suddenly—a gentle breeze.

Who's there . . . ? I sense a presence. And I can hardly believe what comes next. The veins on the leaf begin to twist, curl, and shimmer—a quick pulse of golden light—and those veiny leaf-words scramble and grow larger—larger—larger! Until they magnify into a golden light so bright it blinds me. I put up my hands to block the glare. *What's happening?* I hold my breath.

My heart races. "Show me," I whisper to my crystal. "Hurry." Although I'm whispering, my insides are shaking madly. I command Serpentine:

"Show your power,
throughout this barren land.
Burn brighter, darker
than this little leaf can."

The crystal obeys. Its green, spooky light rises and tries to overtake the blinding sun glare from the little leaf—as if challenging it. The eerie green light from the stone rises up against the gold sheen from the leaf. "That's it! Rise! Rise!" I command my crystal.

Instantly, the two lights begin to collide and swirl into diamond-back shapes: a gold and green reptilian prism. "That's it! That's it!" I urge it on. "Rise! Show your power!" Then my stone's eerie light seeps down like fog into the golden haze and highlights the mysterious words—and before my eyes—unscrambles the peculiar message with supernatural sorcery that reads:

I AM

I'm completely awestruck. *What? I Am? Wha . . . what's this mean?* I can do nothing but marvel in disbelief until I mutter aloud: "I AM?"

Suddenly—as soon as I speak those words, *I Am,*—the breeze blows harder—but it's cool and refreshing. My dirty, black hair becomes a tussle of dark waves blowing in the whooshing breeze.

The wind picks up with greater—greater force!—so much so—it catapults Serpentine from my hands! “No! Serpentine!” I scream. Then to my horror—THWAP!—my stone smashes on the cell floor! A small piece of it breaks off. “NOOOO! SERPENTINE!” I dash forward to pick up my treasured stone. “Thank gosh! Just a small piece broke. I’ll fix you up later,” I pant.

In the mix of all this, as if anything more could happen, the golden light from the leaf begins to outshine the stone’s eerie green glow—my crystal begins to fade. “Don’t leave me. Not now!” I shake it harder. “Don’t leave me, Serpentine. Not now!” But it doesn’t listen. Outshined, Serpentine’s light completely collapses, as if bowing down in defeat to these golden rays in my cell. My stone is dead as a stone. *What’s happening?* I dare not even think! I turn around—and standing in the center of my prison is . . . is . . . *a man!*

With all these goings-on, I barely have time to comprehend. I stare in awe—trying to take this all in. But, being a seer, I can see him. I back into the corner, unsure of what he might do. I examine him. He’s dressed in colors I’ve never seen before, but colors that look like spring, all the way down to his bare feet. Before I can process it all, he’s already at the leaf and watering it with a can. The water sheens a beautiful, sparkly mist in the air.

Who is this man? Did the doorman send him? I watch him as he nurses the plant like a skilled gardener. He has an auburn beard the color of wine. He moves with wonder and grace, and his features are lovely and dignified. Suddenly, and without knowing why, when I look at him, my heart begins to lift like sunshine, for he is glowing.

An illusion? No. I can sense he’s real. Realer than anything I’ve ever felt or seen. I can do nothing but stare at him—completely mesmerized. Suddenly, he turns around and looks directly at me with the kindest, golden-brown eyes I’ve ever seen. And I feel as if this gardener knows me—and that I know him. But from where? I recall the man of light who found me when I was a small child and lost in the dark. My heart pounds out of my chest.

"Be still, my daughter." He smiles. Then he walks toward me and gestures to sit down.

"Who . . . who are you?" I'm unsure of him.

"I Am," he says.

"I Am—who? How did you get in here?"

"I am—*Him.* My father sent me."

"Who's your father?"

"My father owns the gardens, and I tend and prune them."

"In here? In some old, dead forgotten cell?"

"My father is always at work, as I too, am working. Child, there is no time for questions now. Sit, you are protected." He helps me sit down. Then he feels my forehead and wrists. "You are wounded, child," he says. "But do not be afraid." He fetches a cup from a basket and pours the most shimmering, sparkling water from his basin. "Now, drink." He hands me the cup.

I'm *so* thirsty, and without thinking, I drink the entire cup, and after, feel refreshed. Now that he's sitting closer, I take in more of his countenance. He has an extraordinary expression, both serious and lively, so that those who look at him would love him, but at the same time, fear him. He's tall and well-proportioned. His face is without blemish and his cheeks are a light, ruddy color. His appearance is polite and joyful. He has this auburn beard, the same color as his hair, which hangs down below his ears. And his eyes are golden-brown and filled with extreme brilliance.

He takes out a loaf of bread from his basket. "You are hungry, child. Eat this bread." His arms move gracefully as he breaks the bread to feed me.

I hadn't eaten in days. I take the bread and begin to eat. *This bread . . . the most delicious, sweetest bread I've ever had.* I start to feel like new.

"Look," I say between mouthfuls of bread, "I am trying to get out of this place. I've been locked up here. Can you help me?"

"My child, you are in the hour of trial." He speaks kindly but with authority, as if what he says is absolutely true.

"A trial? What do you mean? How do I get out?"

"Gilda, I know you have little strength left. But do not lose hope. I counsel you to take back your crown, and to cover your shame. If you invite me in, I will come in and eat with you."

"How do you know my name?"

"Daughter, I know you. I have known you since the beginning." He takes my hand. The tiny seed-scar in my palm electrifies and pulses gold.

"Is it you? Oh, it is you! You found me when I was lost in the dark as a child!" I stare mesmerized. "All these years, I never forgot you. Oh! You . . . you are real! Do you have a key to this door?"

"Child, I hold the keys to all doors. Listen to me, you must pass this trial—to find release from the darkness of this prison. I will guide the way."

"How?"

"Wake up!" he says. "Waste no more time. Listen with your ears, so you can hear me. And open your eyes, so you can see. You have the gift of visions, but there are things you still must see."

And with that, the breeze starts to blow, and the fresh garden air starts to swirl—swirl—SWIRL—like a new spring—as he begins to vaporize in the wind.

"Wait! Where are you going? How do I get out of here?" I scream in the wind.

"Listen to my voice, child. I will be with you—and counsel you," he assures. His voice echoes in the blast of the breeze as he fades away, and his words strike my heart like glorious thunder, "Open your eyes so you can see! Sin is lurking at your door!" until in the next second—the golden light flashes—and just as quickly as he came—like a thief in the night—he's gone.

CHAPTER TWENTY-FIVE

PRESENT
13 YEARS OLD

Holding cell, Realm of the Dark Night

My thoughts drift to the Quiet Gardener. I feel like I'd been introduced to some god or king: the way he moved with grace, but strong and agile, like a warrior. Being a seer, I felt tremendous power in him. His voice flowed like a bubbling brook but with the force of a thunderous mountain, gentle as a lamb but also strong as a lion. Who *is* this man? This *I AM?* I study the palm of my hand and run my fingers over the tiny seed imprint.

Open your eyes, so you can see. His words play like a chorus in my mind. I stare at the golden veins on the little leaf, these mystery words, no longer a mystery, as they have been decoded as *I AM.*

I Am—who? Agh! So alone in here it's—

"Miss Gilda?"

Oh! It's Abaddon! As if things couldn't get any more chaotic, here *he* is! Ugh.

Strangely, looking at this leaf, a twinge of hope pulses my heart like a flash of sunray. Maybe I could go without the drug I've depended on to breathe? But why should I? I'm not hurting anyone. And oh, the withdrawals . . .

"Miss Gilda? I have your elixir. Can I come in?"

Silence.

"Gilda?"

"I guess." At the sound of his voice, the thousand butterflies swarm. *Why am I feeling this way? I mean, he is a hope for escape.*

He cracks the door. Through the slice of it, his candle illuminates the threshold until the door bursts wide open. His tall, cut body fills the doorway. "Miss Gilda!" He smiles as if he hasn't seen me in years. His black eyes light up, reflecting the fire. Strange, the candle he always has that flickers blue, it looks different this time.

"Is everything OK? May I come inside?"

"You may."

He steps into my cell with a wild flair. His skin gleams, highlighting his dark hair and features. "Here, I brought what you need," he says, "I've been concerned." He hands me the cup of elixir. I stare at it for what seems like eternity—and then—I take it. I hold the drink in my hand. Something feels different.

"I don't know if I want it this time," I say. I turn and stare at the little leaf.

"But you like it, don't you?" He touches the small of my back, as if his mission is to help me. The warmth of his hand sends an unsettling feeling in me. My heart leaps into my mouth. The butterflies awaken and swarm madly inside of me. What do I say? And why do I even care what I say? To some petty doorman. My words lodge in my throat.

"Gilda, come here," he says. He takes the cup and puts it to my lips. "You want to feel free, don't you?" I clutch my chest to hide the hammering of it. The smell of the drug overtakes my senses. Before I can think, I grab it from his hand and gulp it. Within seconds, the tension breaks. Ahhh. I don't fear losing control. I am the master of myself.

He grins. "See, you can be free with me."

Silence. I'm floating.

"You know, I thought you weren't talking to me after—"

"After what?" I stare off.

"Oh, never mind. I thought you might have been upset with me," he says.

Does he sense my feelings? He needs to go.

"Gilda, you seem upset—as if you've been kicked around," he says.

"How do you know what I've been? You know nothing about me."

"Your scars." He takes my hand, looks up and down my arms. "There must be a memory for each one of these," he says, running his fingers over each one.

"Don't look at these up close." I pull my hand back from him.

"Gilda, you're so pretty." His black eyes gaze at me possessively. "I'm sorry, I didn't mean—"

"You should get going," I say, "I'm not feeling too—"

"Gilda, wait. Maybe that's how you can heal . . . maybe we can heal each other's wounds." He takes off his shirt to show the scar on his chest: that three-clawed scar runs through his ink that reads *καταστρέφω*. He points to his scar. "This scar is the sacrifice I paid. I'm not who I am by birth. I fell. And this marking is the reminder for vengeance. My own revenge. We are familiar."

"Revenge on who?"

"On *Him*: a fairytale man who glowed like a god. He was a lie in my head who told me the sun would always come, but never did." His dark eyes narrow. I catch a menacing glare, two black bottomless pits. "I'll never forgive myself for believing my own stupid imagination that brought me pain."

"So, what happened?" I asked.

"It was a lie. The sun never rose for me. For years, I put my trust in a broken promise, false hope. I thought this god was real." He looks away.

"I understand more than you know," I say. "I guess we really are familiar."

"So, what about you?" He faced me. "Wouldn't you like to get them back for those scars?"

"I am. I will," I reply. His words stir that overpowering rage, which had been sleeping until he spoke of it. "If I can get out of this prison. Revenge will settle the score—justice will set me free."

"Vengeance is freedom, Gilda. It's not for the weak to accept these wrongs. It's your assertion of rights. It's your self-worth, as my vengeance is also."

"Well, doomsday is coming—it's coming to those who betrayed to me."

"How can I help?" he asks.

"You can't. These injuries are mine alone to avenge. Besides, it's a risk for you. The one I seek is powerful." I take another drink. "I just need to get out of this damn cell—and find out how the hell I got in here. I have my plan. It's just . . . sometimes I wonder . . . how much anger is too much?"

"By the looks of it," he touches one of my scars, "not enough." He glances at Serpentine, dangling on my chest. "That stone." He toys with it on my chest. "So cold, like you. Oh, I'm sorry, I didn't mean that in a—"

I jerk back my crystal from his grasp.

"Seems like the stone is tapping you into some deeper power—in a strong way," he reassures. "You can't soften at a time like this."

In the mix of all this, with his body close to mine, and my anger and our connection for freedom and pains we acknowledge but don't entirely speak of, I know I've never felt this intimate with anyone. So intimate I could throw up. But he makes me feel that I have no scars—he doesn't see my wounds. He sees *me.*

"So, what's your story?" he asks.

"I was kidnapped at eight years old."

"And these scars?"

"Only one scar is from my twin sister, from Sunbeam, but it's the deepest one and invisible to the eye. All the others are from Wolford, the one who took me. Years in captivity, in his cave, and when she—Sunbeam—crossed the Depths of Cypress, and into The Valley of Dry Bones, the place where that demon hid me, she was selfish . . . never even bothered to see about me. She left me there to rot . . . to die. And Wolford, the devil himself, when he realized he took the wrong twin, told me the only way he'd spare my life and set me free was if I captured her. 'Bring Sunbeam to me, and you go free,'" he offered.

"But why? Why did he want her in the first place? And then you?"

"He said she was the One Called. That we both had been given power. We were a threat to his mission to destroy Ozmandia, the island where I lived. So, Wolford said either we join him, or die. 'This is a war between the gods,' he'd say. 'Soon, all will be clear. I will stretch my hand and have Ozmandia and all the cities around, to enlighten the minds of men away from the God of Lights. And you will serve me, or sleep forever,' he'd hiss, sharpening his claw. This terrible claw he had. You probably wouldn't believe me if I told you, but I'll tell you anyway. Have you ever read those old mythical stories on gods? Well, it's real. I know this is a war between the gods. It's in a higher realm. I know this because I've seen it. I am a seer. I can astral travel across dimensions . . . across time and space. And apparently, Sunbeam and I have the powers he wants. But for some reason, he initially wanted her, not me. I assume he thought she was more of a threat. I do have my gifts but need out of this prison to fully use them. Something is keeping me stuck."

"Don't be weak, Gilda."

"Do I look weak?" I laugh. "Lambs don't defeat wolves. Only wolves defeat wolves."

"So, how did you get taken?" he asks.

"Sunbeam. Sunbeam's games. We used to swap identities for fun. As twins, no one could tell us apart, and we thought it was funny. One night, she made me play, but I didn't want to that night. I had a bad feeling. But she forced me to—kept on and on. And if we hadn't swapped identities that night to trick our new nanny, that demon would have taken *her*, not me. I was sleeping in her bed, and she, in mine. And the devil took me out of Sunbeam's bed, thinking I was her. Now don't get me wrong, it's not as if I wanted my own twin taken, but it's that she hasn't cared one bit that I was. It's her fault. And even more, Wolford kept calling me Sunbeam, so I felt revealing my identity would endanger me. Until five years later—he found out the truth."

'Your twin is the One Called? I've taken the wrong one!' he bellowed and growled. 'All these years, you've hidden your identity!' he shouted and hissed over and over with his claw scratching my flesh, furious after he was slapped with the truth. See, I pretended to be Sunbeam for fear I'd lose my life."

"How'd he find out the truth?"

"He discovered who I was after Sunbeam came to the Depths, and when he saw her, Sunbeam fled. My own twin left me. Coward! She abandoned me. 'You would already be dead if I weren't using you for bait!' Wolford roared. And after a slew of more 'You're the wrong one!' and 'Liar!' and 'You will pay for this deceit!' he decided on a deal. 'Now,' he turned to me and growled, 'the only way to redeem this wrong is that you serve me and—end her—so you may live. Unless, dear Gilda, Sunbeam willingly gives herself in exchange. She has limited time! And in that time, it'll either be you—or her. Let's see how much your beloved twin cares for you,' he smirked. 'I am sending your locket with the golgums to her as proof. When she opens the letter and sees the locket, she'll know you're in my possession.

If she comes to retrieve you, then you'll know she cares. If not, shouldn't she die anyway? Leaving *you* here for dead?'"

"So, did she come for you?"

"He sent the locket to her. His minions, golgums, tracked her down and delivered it to her in a letter. She . . . she took the locket, the last thing she ever gave me, and threw the locket in the river. And she left the Depths: left me and the locket behind—the last thing linking me to her. She tossed it away like an old rag."

"I'm so sorry, Gilda. I, too, know the sting of betrayal and abandonment."

"And that's not it. My father. My own father: number 277181958."

"Gilda, if this is too much to—"

"No! It's out now. He . . . he was in the cave, the place Wolford hid me for years. I saw him. One night, I woke to a looming shadow and saw his face flash by in the pit. But I dismissed it and thought I was just seeing things. Then later, he came into my dungeon disguised, where I was hidden and would talk to me. A mask covered his face, so I never knew it was my own father. Then after many nights of talking, one night he came in and woke me from a dead sleep wearing the mask.

'Gilda,' he said. 'Gilda, I'm your father!'

'How do you know my name?' I said. I was still posing as Sunbeam and sprang up in shock. My heart was pounding. He pulled off his mask to show his face. At first, I hardly recognized him, unsure of who he was until I realized he was my father, gazing at me as if he had lost his way, but just found himself. 'Gilda, I'm your father,' he whispered frantically. 'Gilda, I'm so sorry. I'm your father.' Then he took me. I thought he was there to rescue me. He carried me out of the cave—he was running me through the forest under moonlight. I asked him, 'Why? Father, why am I here? Why are you here?'

'I'm redeeming what I've done—what I've done to you. The mistake I made,' he cried.

'What have you done?' I pleaded.

"But he wouldn't answer. He just stared ahead, running with me as fast as he could go . . . until . . . until Wolford tracked and found us, and beat my father severely. I cried, 'Father! What is happening? Tell me! And where is Sunbeam?' But he collapsed from the beating without one word, until they carried him off. And that was the last time I spoke to him. But my father was a master in magic and escapology. So I assume he escaped.

"Being a seer, I saw one last flash of him. He was in the Depths with Sunbeam. Together. Those two—together—while I lay chained in darkness. And what pressed me down even more wasn't the darkness itself, but the confusion in it—and the bafflement of abandonment. All I wanted to know was *why*. I wanted truth. But I never got answers. Just complete silence and a pit to sit and stew while they ran about, not bothering to find me, nor see if I was alive."

"I don't understand."

"Neither do I. But I do understand that some questions go unanswered, and we must draw our own conclusions. I've drawn mine. They did what they did. I saw what I saw. They discarded me—cast me off like a dirty old rag—and left scars that go deeper and are more agonizing than anything that bleeds. Lawbreakers!"

"Gilda, I'm not going to leave you in here." He takes my hand. "They say you can bury the past, but like you, I know that's wrong. Because the past claws its way back up."

"Yah, here I am. No longer in that devil's dungeon, but I'm still peering back into that hellhole. I don't know how I got here. But I know it's connected. I just woke up in this cell. 'You or her,' he hissed. 'If she doesn't return, this will be your end' were the last words I heard. And while waiting for Sunbeam—poof! I woke up here nine months ago. I don't know why or whether my silver cord is intact or if it's been cut. This cell blocks complete understanding. I just know time is running out. These walls are closing in. I must get free."

"You're not alone," he leans closer.

In the heat of all this, I find it hard to catch my breath, not because of my anger, but because of his sudden proximity. Then he hugs me, and holding me tightly, he smells so good with that mixed scent of jasmine and leather on his skin. He grips me harder. And honestly, he feels so familiar and comforting. This is the type of friendship I've wanted since he entered my cell. *But really? Do I?*

"You need to go." I pull away. I shake it off and try to slow my heart.

"Gilda, you can be free with me. Here." He tips the drug to my lips again. I drink. "See, now you have peace." He leans in closer and pins me with a direct gaze, his black eyes possessing every part of me. At this point, it's as though he sees past all my insecurities. "You're quite . . . amazing," he whispers. He tucks my hair behind my ear. "You have such a pretty face." And then . . . he kisses me. And oh, my stars! I have *never* been kissed by anyone before. Have you ever seen one of those paintings of an angel—some perfect celestial being rushing down to save you? That's how it feels when he kisses me. It's more than a kiss, it's something unworldly.

"I'll be your rock," he says. His voice is like velvet.

His strong arms wrap around me. We are so close in the firelight; I see only small patches of his glistening skin. I have never felt so close with anyone else—ever!

"I don't want anything to come between us," he whispers. "No boundaries. Nothing. Tell me, do you want that?"

"I . . . I . . ." His skin is smooth against mine. His lips taste like salty mint.

"Your skin is glowing," he says.

My heart pounds in the wonder of his minty kisses. He is even more strikingly good-looking than ever.

"Under these gloomy, terrible circumstances, I'm so glad I found you," he says. Heat rages between us, a tension close to exploding like fireworks. We sit and talk all night. At this point I'm lying on my side, elbow propped under my ear, listening to every word he speaks. The air is a thick fog, sweet as candy. My jet-black hair is fanned across my mat as he sits across from me, curious about every part of my life.

"I want to stay like this forever." He smiles. In this moment, he makes me feel so . . . so adored.

"Gilda, you know, maybe we don't know our worth until it's reflected through the eyes of another person. I can't ever imagine feeling like this with anyone else."

I never have, I think to myself. I hate that I suddenly feel like he knows what to say, and I don't.

"I'm beginning to understand you, Gilda." He hugs me, and we remain embraced until . . .

He spots the green plant growing up through the crack in my cell. He freezes. His entire body stiffens. He breathes a little faster. His chest tattoo—καταστρέφω—moves up and down as his eyes widen like he's seen a *terrible* surprise. He sits up and stares at the leaf. "Miss Gilda, what is that?"

Long silence.

"These old weeds need to be removed." He walks briskly to pull up the plant.

"No! Leave it," I say.

"This is nothing but an old weed," he warns, "It could be poisonous!" He attempts to pull it out of the concrete, but the leaf doesn't uproot. His arm muscles bulge trying to rip out the only life in my cell.

"Leave it!" It's not a weed!" I command.

He dismisses my words. Sweat breaks out on his forehead. "Come on!" He continues pulling and yanking. But the plant remains firm and rooted, as if the strongest of all men couldn't cut it down.

In the next second, he whips around to face me, as if searching for any hint of betrayal. "Gilda, has anyone else been in this cell?"

"Abaddon, I'm not going to hurt you," I say.

His eyes, two piercing arrows, which only moments ago gazed at me with adoration, are now darker and more bottomless than I've ever seen. So dark, that a twinge of caution awakens my senses. And as he stands blocking the only life growing in my cell, the quiet gardener's words suddenly strike me like muted thunder: *Open your eyes, so you can see.*

CHAPTER TWENTY-SIX

GILDA

PRESENT
13 YEARS OLD

Holding cell, Realm of the Dark Night

Now alone, I stare at the small plant. I run my fingers over its spring petals. A strange paradox, this little leaf: soft as a whisper, but stable as a rock. Despite Abaddon's pulling and yanking and his "It's poisonous!" and striking it like a scorpion, "It's an old weed!" and baring his teeth, "Get rid of it!"—it never budged. Not once.

Why had Abaddon wanted it out of here? He looked menacing . . . scary really . . . like a different person.

I recall the marking on his chest. *How strange.* After more study, I realize the lettering on his marking matches the lettering on this leaf. It's written in the same mysterious language.

"What's it mean? Show me, Serpentine."

I clutch my crystal. My heart hardens. My soul screams; then comes rushing waves of high and low and the yesterday and today and—I swallow what's left of the elixir—and reliably, ever so reliably, my stone lights slime-green on the prison wall—*show me—yes, no, not again, nooo . . . nooooo!*—until it casts me into another dark nightmare of my past.

CHAPTER TWENTY-SEVEN

GILDA

PAST
YEARS AGO

Valley of Dry Bones

It had been five long years I was prisoner in the valley. I was thirteen years old when Wolford found out my identity, that I was Gilda, *not* Sunbeam. And after his offer for me to capture Sunbeam, and bring her to him, I agreed.

I had already discovered the extent of my powers: astral traveling to dimensions unknown. I soared into realms dismissed by most people, and by "most" I mean those types who deny anything spiritual or dismiss anything beyond what the human eye can see. You know the type, they see the ocean as a body of molecules rather than its heavenly sunsets, its magical mysteries and wonder that stir a young, adventurous mind.

"How am I a villain, dear Gilda?" hissed Wolford. "Do I not counsel you on this dark course for your direct good? Your own appetite drives you." He ran the tip of his claw down my cheek. "I unlock you, let you roam free in the Valley and ethereal planes—to bring Sunbeam, your betrayer—to me. Child, there are times you must commit evil for your own good."

"Where is my father? What have you done with him? And why was he here?"

"I told you over and over, child. You needn't worry about that now."

"Is he alive?"

"Your father gave his soul to devilish pursuits! He is a high-class hostage."

Wolford stood tall, his Guild of Golgums loyally behind him in their long, black cloaks, those lifeless minions, bowing and nodding in approval at his every word like scared mice. Then, he turned to face them, "On your knees, every one of you, to your prince!" He raised his claw.

"Oh master, to hear is to obey, to hear is to obey," they all whined and fell on their knees. "And now, you fools, marvel at this girl who is stronger than all of you. I should run a dagger through all of you right now for your incompetence, for your weakness!"

"Well, if it weren't for them, you'd have no army," I smirked. "You've lived on nothing but broken hearts your whole existence." I didn't care how I spoke to the tyrant. He needed me. He wouldn't kill me . . . not yet.

Wolford walked slowly toward me, put his claw under my chin, and hissed, "I'll be glad when I have you off my hands—although that lovely bitterness in you is the fire that will bring the One Called to me." He smiled menacingly.

"You know what to do, little wolf," he snarled. "Do not forget my command, when you ascend, never—*never* leave your silver cord vulnerable. If your cord is broken, the door to life is closed." Then he turned and disappeared into the cave, his guild crawling behind him with a slew of "Oh, your majesty" and "To hear is to obey, to hear is to obey."

❧ ❧

I was alone. I walked out of the mazy darkness, lantern in hand. I came to the end. Vengy slithered next to my feet. "You have done well, Vengy. You helped me accomplish my spells, and we will always be together. But now, I must go after Sunbeam myself," I said.

"Oh, misssss, I will be right here when you come back. I am hungry."

The moonlight shone into the mouth of the cave. I stopped at the opening of it. I had to bring Sunbeam to him, or that dungeon would be *my* end.

I knew she was powerful, like me. This wouldn't be easy. And what's more, there was Whitewing, my loyal, sweet horse, whom I hadn't seen since I was taken. I wondered if he missed me. I knew she was riding horseback on him through the Depths. After much magic, I had finally sensed her location in one of my seeing spells, but still needed to find her in real time.

Maybe we can both escape? I don't want her or Whitewing harmed. I just want justice and freedom. Why? Why has this fallen into my lap?

The thought of it all made me sick. But then again, she'd left me for dead. What did I owe her? With the *Book of Shadows* in one hand, I took a big swig of the elixir with the other, to numb the painful surge swirling in my heart.

It was urgent. I had to act. A seer, I braced for ascent. It was time.

I'm going to find her. I sense she's close.

Do not cut your silver cord, or the door to life will close forever. Wolford's words played over and over in my head like a mantra—because when you astral project, your silver cord brings your soul back to your body—and if cut—you're good as dead—lost in a celestial black hole for eternity. Separate from soul and body. And you're either left stranded on the astral plane or killed both physically and astrally.

Thinking of this, for a long time I dared not move. Could this be that devil's trick to lure me to my doom? Floating in some black abyss, all alone forever? But I couldn't ponder this all night. I had to act. I took a step closer to the mouth of the cave, which opened into the Depths of Cypress: a mystical place between two worlds, between our world and theirs: humans and gods.

The silver moonlight lit a landscape of trees that seemed to go on forever. I tried to get my breath. This would be a new world. I wondered how well I'd travel. I took another swig of my drug to melt the guilt of what I was about to do. I opened the *Book of Shadows*.

I set my intent. My eyelids were closed. Ready to astral travel, I began the mantra:

"Midnight moon,
I will rise
owning the dark
open your skies.

"On this black and hexing night,
spread your wings—Unhinge!
for blood and Justice, and for Revenge!"

With the elixir relaxing me, and the help of dark magic as the best vengeance, higher sensations began to flow through my muscles until my consciousness began to leave my body. I was being swept into a faraway place. The world became dim as I climbed my silver cord into that higher realm. In the next moment, I was floating above my body and looking down on myself. Higher—higher I ascended—until the places where the moonlight fell clear on the ground displayed two shadowed wings beside me. *What on earth?*

The shadows on the ground, two large wings—they moved when I moved. When I moved to the right, that side of the wing moved—and when left—the same side moved! For a second, this was so alarming I held my breath. This would be enough to scare anyone! But I dare not descend. I could not turn back.

"Spread your wings—Unhinge!
In the name of Justice, and for Revenge!"

Then, with all my might, I made a bolt upward and—to my great shock—I let out a scream deep within me—but it wasn't a scream—it was a strange noise I'd never made before. It sounded like a CAW. The sound a majestic and glorious bird makes when it's shooting across the sky. *What the . . . wha . . . ?* And then I knew I had reached it. I was carried into the astral plane!

And what came next is unfathomable! For when I looked down, my vision was keener and clearer than ever before, and when I soared over a large river, it all came over me and made sense. I realized the truth. For when I looked down upon the water, I saw my reflection. And there was no doubt of it—lo and behold—I had transformed into a bird! A large, terrifying black scavenger with wings that seemed to spread out as far as the east is from the west. I had done it! I had crossed through the dimension of time and space and was soaring like a great fowl!

Freedom! I soared and soared under a full moon that lit trees, rivers, and landscape which stretched out for miles and miles. And what's more, all my senses became sharp and clear, but inside I felt void of human sensitivities. Astral projecting with a heart of rage and scavenger thoughts, I had become a scavenger myself: ready to devour. A sharp-eyed raptor with a black heart and vulture instincts. And oh! You should have seen me fly—with perfect precision—the most skilled aerialist. I owned the sky.

And oh! What relief I had! Because there was nothing to fear. I was a terror to all. Nothing in the world would dare stop me—nor lock me up! I was a beast of prey to be reckoned with! And now, I could get even with Sunbeam.

But then in the same moment, it dawned on me I didn't want to be a scavenger forever—cut off from all mankind, wandering lonely as a bird—and this sudden loneliness drove my wings into a wild rage of flapping. My wingspan stretched in fury. My mission was just beyond the field of vision. I had to catch my prey, my betrayer, and fly her back to Wolford. Then, I would be free. And I could return to the human race, back home, and live again.

Time and space beckoned as I soared through the planes in search of Sunbeam. I soared and soared for a long while into the night: trees, moon, river, leaves—but did not see her.

Finally, to my surprise, I spotted movement way down below. I swooped lower to get a better look from the sky.

And then, my marble eye spotted her! *Oh! Could it really be her? All this time!* My heart pounded, and I realized it was beating faster than ever. *Is this the excitement a vulture feels when it spots prey on the ground?*

She was sleeping on a little bed of leaves. There were two other children beside her, a boy, and a girl, about my age. *Those must be her friends. I don't have friends. So, she's building a social life while I'm stuck in a hole?*

I had to move quickly. But then it struck me, where was Whitewing? With my sharp bird's eye view, I zoomed in and found my beloved horse a little distance off, having grass and a drink at a small stream. I had to act immediately. I pushed all my human thoughts to the back of my mind, bracing myself to be savage, like the bird I was. And being in the right celestial sphere—at just the right time—I dove down through the dimensions of time and space—directly upon her. I dug my talons into the back of her collar.

"Wha—wha?!" She stirred, yawned, then went to shouting. "Scat! You wretched thing! Get!" I covered her mouth with my large talons. Sunbeam swatted and kicked. Oh, had she known that it was I, Gilda, her own flesh and blood—not a vulture that had her. And then I realized, at the same time she wiggled in my talons, I was also pecking at the ground to eat the crumbs from her leftover biscuit. *What the . . . ?* And this was so bizarre I almost laughed—and realized although I was thinking like a human, my tastes and instincts were scavengerish. And there's nothing a fowl likes more than breadcrumbs. And then I snapped to, and wildly, shot upward, soaring her through the dark sky.

"Let me go! Get!" Sunbeam swatted at the air. And then I noticed a key dangling around her neck and flashing gold. *How strange. A key?* But I dismissed it from my mind. It didn't matter what door that key opened because she'd be locked up soon with no way out, and no key would open that devil's door once locked inside the most wicked sorcery. Yes, she was a ragdoll in my large, glorious talons, squirming through the sky, soon to be dropped in the doom that chained *me* the last five years, but the destiny *she* deserved all along.

After a long stretch of flying through more clouds, stars, and a silver skyline, I reached the cave: Wolford's coven of black arts. I heard the devil already calling as I descended from a high altitude. I began slowing to enter the mouth of the cave.

"Let me go!" Sunbeam shouted and flailed the whole way, trying to tear herself loose. But nothing could tear her from my grip. You should have seen me—ascending, swooping and gliding—a horrific splendor before all.

I narrowed my sharp, raptor eye on the cave opening, stretched my black wings, dove down—then entered.

Zooming through the mazy, narrow passages, I pulled my wings all the way back like a bullet—until I reached the coven. There, deep in the cave, Wolford sat on his throne, slamming his claw and berating his golgums: "Dirty, filthy sychophants! You dare let a weak girl destroy my work? I should come down and run ten of you through at a time with one thrust into your cold, worthless bodies for your lack of skill!"

The golgums raised their faces like dogs to look up at him and chanted: "Oh master, may you be lifted high, though we are destroyed. To hear is to obey. To hear is to obey."

The deal was only to exchange Sunbeam for myself. Why all the fuss? The "fuss" I mean was a table where other golgums slid around it in unison like a dance. They were sprinkling red dust on it with their grey, wrinkled hands. *What was going on?* I almost doubted whether to leave Sunbeam. What was the table for? And why such a spectacle? But before I could think, my scavenger-ish pride reminded me if I let my prey go, my prey might strike me, as all prey does when trying to escape the grip of its predator. And then I remembered she'd already struck me—that was her last blow.

In fury, I bellowed like a battle horn in the cave, so loud it shook the walls. I had done it. I had brought my beloved to him. I would finally be free.

In the mix of all this, as I flew, Wolford gazed and showcased me in front of the guild, as though I was his airshow of haunting, glorious pride. "If not for the great wandering scavenger," he shouted, "she might have gotten away! Servile buffoons! Even this vulture is swifter than all of you. Now, you shall bear witness to this high matter." He stabbed his claw at the air. "Oh, Great Wandering Scavenger, bring me this . . . One Called."

I hated to admit it, but for a second my heart winced. I was about to break the agreement at the thought of leaving Sunbeam in that demon's clutches. *Lambs don't defeat wolves. Only wolves defeat wolves,* ran over and over in my mind. I circled for a long moment in the air contemplating my next move until . . . until *in the name of justice, and for revenge!* snapped me back to the reality of what she'd done. My god, she'd left me for dead.

And pushing all my sensitivities to the back of my black wings, I descended with terrorizing bellows that only the largest fowl can make when it's caught prey—and once in its talons, nothing . . . nothing can get in its way. And swooping to drop Sunbeam with that jackal, one of the golgums yelled, "Look at the fire reflecting in the Great Scavenger's eye! Triumphant!"

"CAW! CAW!" I shrieked.

Lord Wolford slammed his claw on his throne. "Bring her before me."

At the order, rage raised my feathers. I opened my beak and let out another scream that sounded like a siren until I'd reached Wolford's throne. I opened my large wings and stopped in mid-air, dangling Sunbeam directly in front of him so that only a small space was between them.

Everything went silent. Everyone waited for the next move. Before Wolford spoke a word, he started waving his claw in circles. And the golgums below began crooning hexing chants, but what came next was unfathomable! I suddenly lost my hearing. Everything went completely mute. Despite Wolford's lips moving and Sunbeam's eyebrows scrunched and her raising her fist to him, I could not hear a word! What were they saying? What was Sunbeam shouting? And why had I lost my hearing? The whole scene was a silent movie playing out, so I could only assume the plot. And by the looks of it, Sunbeam was furious that she'd been caught. After a long moment, suddenly, POOF! My hearing returned and was tuning into Wolford's voice, which commanded me, "Great wandering scavenger! Go forth! Wait and watch." He winked at me with a gleam in his blue eye. I mean, I wouldn't have followed that jackal's order unless it was for our plan. Naturally, this was part of the plan, to make the exchange, me for her. I swished downward from the ceiling and flew out.

Oh! Hunger surged through my vulture veins. The hunger I knew would soon be quelled. After five long years, Sunbeam would stand before me. She would have to face her forgotten twin—eye to eye. The exchange would soon be official. And Sunbeam would see me, not as this scavenger, but as Gilda. My plan was to shift back to my human self once she entered. And oh! I wondered what she might say to me as she looked at every one of my scars, her twin, and had to face what she'd done. I could imagine it! She'd see that I'd won! I'd be free—while this time she stayed behind—and I'd leave her—like she left me. And next, I would deal with Father. I'd get all the answers. Yes, in the name of justice, and for revenge.

CHAPTER TWENTY-EIGHT

GIL'DA

PAST
YEARS AGO

Valley of Dry Bones

It had been a long wait. I'd found myself nibbling on crumbs from the ground. With no more crumbs to peck, time lingered. *Look at me!* I thought. Horrified, there was no way I would let anyone catch me searching for crumbs like some grimy old fowl. Wolford needed to hurry. The vulture slowly consumed me more and more.

Where was Sunbeam? Surely it couldn't take this long. I waited in the dungeon where he kept me captive for five long years. My dungeon: that was the meeting place. There, we'd make the exchange. It was the perfect spot for Sunbeam to see the hellhole where she'd left me and what would soon be her new home. I waited and waited . . . until I'd waited long enough. *Where was that demon? Surely, he wouldn't go back on the plan.* I'd done my job. Brought my betrayer to him. *Where in the—*

Just as I was about to fly back to the coven, Wolford burst through the entrance like a mad prince, his pathetic guild trailing behind him in their cloaks like one long, black train. One of them was whining, "Oh master, we should be utterly destroyed for this. May you be lifted high! And us destroyed!"

Wolford stopped. He turned toward me, staring at me with his eyes like blue ice. Silence overtook the cave until he hissed, "She's gone! Gone. Gone!"

As soon as he said *gone* my insides sunk.

Then Wolford turned and pointed his claw to his groveling, cloaked army, "Turn your dogged faces aside! Do not dare look at me until you have retrieved her!"

The golgums bowed, and a slew of frantic "To hear is to obey, to hear is to obeys," filled the cave.

What stopped all this was a terrible sound that came out the bottom of my soul. And right then, I knew what a real vulture felt like—without any human thoughts to rethink a course of action—just sheer animal instinct—and scavenger filth! It was time to fight dirty. I pulled my wings back as far as they would go, let out another awful bellow that shook the whole cave, and flew out like a terrible storm.

"That's it! Fly, Gilda! Fly! Show her who you are! Fly!" Wolford's voice echoed as I whooshed through the opening of the cave. I howled and opened my beak wide and glared up to the moon—a skilled hunter of the night—vowing Sunbeam would soon be back in my hooks.

But this time—I wasn't bringing her back to Wolford—this time—would be her *last* time.

❧ ❧

I soared and hunted for a long stretch. For what seemed like eternity, I flew and flew until, lo and behold, I spotted a few moving specks where some moonlight fell below. Immediately, I descended. You see, I had to make sure it wasn't a pack of wild hyaenas or some other four-legged creatures. As soon as the altitude lessened, it was confirmed: Sunbeam! And also running were those strange friends accompanying her, the boy and girl about my age. And my father! Father? *What on earth?* All running madly through the Depths.

In less than a second, I swiftly dove. I was upon Sunbeam! Before she could think, I'd sunk my hooks into her collar, circled, and snatched her straight up into the black horizon.

"Cunning snake!" my father yelled from below, shaking his fist.

Oh, had he known it was me—his own daughter—Gilda!

Sunbeam, completely out of reach from their grabbing hands, dangled like a ragdoll under the silver moon. I turned wing and flew as fast as a vulture can fly. This time—she was mine.

I looked down with my vulture eye. My father ran alongside Sunbeam's two friends, the boy and girl, who shrank smaller the further I ascended. I saw the boy jump on Whitewing's back. I lost them as they ran on land and disappeared through the trees. But strangely, the girl locked eyes with me. Despite her distance from the ground, it was as if she could read my animal instinct. In a second, she waved her hands into the air. Then with my sharp hearing, I heard her call loudly:

"Oh feathered ones,
who flock the skies,
bring this scavenger
down to size!"

This girl is casting a spell! If anyone knew magic, it was me. *Oh, don't play with me, you little twit! You're no match for me!* I thought. I ascended at rapid speed. But in the next moment, to my shock, a drove of bright-winged eagles shot across the Eastern Sky. Their shrieks echoed across the horizon. They extended their wings and hovered above me, covering like a winged battalion to block me from ascending higher. And that strange girl below kept waving her hands, directing the eagles. *Little twit! She's called in some eagles!* I pulled back my wings and shot through the trees. After a stretch, I broke through and ascended higher into the open sky.

But then what came next was the most appalling! For soaring through the air at great speed, something was flying directly at me from the center of the moon. Then, the thing streaked across the sky like a gleaming comet.

I zoomed in with my vulture eye. *Wha . . . ?* It was a horse—large and pearlescent white, with a wingspan as wide, if not wider, than mine. On its back rode a boy about my age—thirteen. I picked up speed. Locking into me with his large, round eyes, the white horse let out a battle scream that rang across the sky. It sounded like a horn or a great trumpet. And I looked closer to find that—to my utter horror—it wasn't just a horse—it was *my* horse! Whitewing! Soaring through the sky like a gleaming arrow with that boy on his back, and the boy was trembling and completely white in the face.

The boy's eyes were wide as saucers. And he was saying something. I tuned in to hear. See, as a scavenger, your eye is much sharper than a human's. You can see from far-off distances and hear perceptibly well. So, although flying, I could also listen closely.

"Hold on, boy! Ride! That's it! Ride!" shouted Whitewing to the boy, as if giving him a riding lesson. And it was then I almost flipped my wing—for my old horse was not only flying—but talking? Whitewing could talk in the Depths! Oh! If Whitewing only knew it was me, Gilda! I melted at the sight of him. He was a good horse. I loved him.

"Now!" Whitewing shouted to the boy in blasts of wind, "I'm going to pick up speed, and you're going to grab Sunbeam's heels and pull her down onto my back!"

I should have known. Whitewing, a loyal horse, would protect Sunbeam. He was coming to save her. But I never dreamed of anything like this: my horse zipping through the clouds like a glimmering spear!

"Help me, Harmon! Hurry, Whitewing!" Sunbeam shouted. She wriggled in my hooks. Yet, she looked just as shocked as

I did that our horse was shooting across the sky like a pearl-white arrow. And in that same moment, I remembered the tale of the flying warhorses and that father brought him to us when we were little because he was too small to be a warhorse. So, the stablemen sold him for cheap. But by the look of it, he flew with supreme skill, whipped and jerked at just the right moments, like a swinging blade or a battleax—not just a warhorse—a *flying* warhorse. And in that same moment, I saw the stablemen weren't telling some old fairytale about flying warhorses. They'd always told it like it was a myth, and yet, it wasn't a myth at all. It was the realest moment I'd ever beheld.

Then I realized the worst thing. It fell over me like the darkest cloud as I soared through that full moon. Since I wouldn't be setting Sunbeam free . . . I . . . I'd have no other choice—would I have to fight Whitewing?

And for a moment, a fire flared through me, but not a fire that I'd known before, but the fire of a dark vulture about to lose control.

After more flying, twists and turns through the clouds, and Whitewing keeping pace underneath my talons in the flight, it wasn't easy to escape. But there wasn't a chance I'd let some riled-up friend of hers riding Whitewing get in my way. Nothing was taking my ticket out of hell. I shot forward and shrieked wildly. By the look on their faces, they must have thought me a dark mass of terror. I tried to scare Whitewing away, so he'd turn and leave, to keep him safe. All I wanted was justice: drop Sunbeam without injury—and go.

To my shock, he didn't flinch but raised his wings and whooshed with great force to catch up. He was good. Too good. Even more, that boy's fear vanished from his face. He'd stopped trembling, and his color returned. And he, too, fell into the rhythm of the race.

"That's it, son! Ride!" shouted Whitewing in blasts of wind. "Pull, boy! Pull!"

I looked down. *You puny little giglet!* I thought. For the boy had leapt into the small space of air, catching Sunbeam by her heel. Then, sharp blasts of wind rushed by me like whizzing arrows! *What was that noise?* I'll tell you; the boy was trying to strike my wing with a flute he'd pulled from his belt loop! *What in the name of—! Not now, you wretched vex!*

This only surged more fire through my wings. I shot upward. But to my shock, the boy latched onto Sunbeam's heel. Both of them dangled in a heap from my talons as I blasted through the night sky. *Some overly devoted friend he was!* This was between me and Sunbeam, not him. Not anyone else. I wanted only her.

The weight of them both on my talons unsteadied me. I swiveled about the air. Lashing insults at the nuisance-boy, my insults rang out, not as human words, but as "CAWWW!" *I'll drop altitude,* I thought. *I have to get this surly little varlet off my talons.*

"Let her go, you beast! Drop her!" the boy yelled, swinging his flute.

Sorry, kid, but it's come to this. I lurched my head underbelly, trying to peck the boy's eyes out with my beak. Relentless as he was, I had no choice. He was trying to kill me! In the tempo of the flight, a second from taking him out, suddenly, something felt as if it *bit* me!

"CAWWWW!" I reared back in severe pain. To my horror, it wasn't a bite, it was the nuisance's flute! He'd struck me with such a heavy blow I unsteadied and curled backward.

"You got the thing, Harmon! You did it!" Sunbeam shouted in terrified glee.

I wobbled in pain. This caused me to lose my grip: and this was the second the boy and my betrayer needed to get away. They dropped through the air and—THUD!—landed on Whitewing's back.

"That's it, boy! Ride! That's it!" shouted Whitewing to the nuisance like a proud coach. Then without warning, Whitewing dove down like a glimmering, pearl sword swiping downward through the air. He was heading toward land.

Noooooo! That little rogue friend of hers! I wasn't going back without Sunbeam. You see, nothing can take prey from a raptor's talons. Now a vulture, I felt vultureish, and ready to do anything a vulture would do to survive. I was a mix of two winged creatures, like a raptor-vulture: a wonderous, majestic nighthawk sprinkled with a fouled-up scavenger. Skilled and marvelous in the sky, but dirty as a scavenger on the ground and ready to fight that way. A filthy vulture that would devour anything crossing its path.

I slicked back my wings and rushed toward them. I could feel my eyes glare like two red flames. My wings spiked like daggers as I swooped down after them: a whizzing arrow, cutting through the air. I thrust my razor-sharp beak toward the boy, that nuisance blocking my freedom.

I'd caught up. I flew at Whitewing's heels. But every time I aimed and lunged at the boy, Whitewing would burst forward, and I'd miss the boy, accidentally stabbing Whitewing's hind legs with my beak, which was tearing his flesh. *Dammit! That nuisance boy caused me to injure my horse!*

"Fly, Whitewing!" Sunbeam cried. "It's on us! It's tearing into you! Oh, it's my fault! I should have tied you up!" she screamed.

In the next second, Whitewing dove and reduced altitude. I knew he was trying to descend closer to land. Both Sunbeam and the nuisance craned their necks backward to get a look, trying to see how close I trailed behind them. Wide creases splayed across their foreheads in terrified lines. Their eyes were large and gleaming in a patch of silver moon. They both held tightly onto his back.

"Fly Whitewing, Fly! It's close behind! The thing's catching up!" shouted Sunbeam. At her order, Whitewing picked up speed and flew fast as lightning; he became a tiny white speck the further he descended.

I went down after him.

Did you think I'd be this easy? I thought.

It didn't take long for me to catch up. But when I did, Whitewing had already slowed speed, skimming close to the ground. *Was he making a landing?* I braced. Instantly, both Sunbeam and the nuisance boy with the flute leapt off his back and rolled in the grass like two tumbleweeds. "Whitewing!" Sunbeam screamed. "You are not to fight it! I'll tie you up!"

He's let them off, I thought. *Here's my chance.* I dove for Sunbeam.

"CAW! CAW!" I was a second from hooking her! But to my shock, I found myself tumbling backwards into the moon! *Whaaat in the name of—?*

It was Whitewing! He'd blocked my aim. Just before retrieving my betrayer, my own Whitewing had kicked like a horse into my underbelly, a ferocious warhorse, and sent me flailing headlong into to the sky.

By the time I gained my bearings, he'd already come up after me.

At this height, nothing was heard except the scattering of the four winds. We were eye to eye, wing to wing. Suddenly, I realized we had a crowd watching us from the clouds. For the bright-winged eagles swooshed overhead, looking upon us like spectators from the heavens. Every eye above and below was now locked onto me and my beloved horse. It was the most dreadful feeling—facing my own beloved Whitewing in combat!

Only one would own the sky that night—and determined not to be locked up—I *would* win this fight.

Maybe I could make it so Whitewing got away with just a scratch or a nick on his hide, but no, both of his wings were stretched across the sphere like swords, and by the look in his warhorse eye—I knew he didn't come up with one wing in—like me—he had come to win.

❧ ❧

I'm going to end him. Wait. No. But . . . maybe I can let him off with just a scratch. I only had to keep my silver cord. Do not sever your silver cord, Wolford's voice warned, *or the door to life closes forever.*

I opened my wings.

I didn't want it to come this, but that fire that flared through me earlier—the fire of a dark vulture about to lose control—was taking over. I was losing all control.

In the name of Justice, and for Revenge! NOW!

I darted for his face. Before I could think, a strong force possessed me—all raptor—I struck him again like a serpent in the air. The vulture in me zipped and circled, a pristine aerial acrobat, pecking at his bit to shoo him. There was nothing but wings, hoofs, and teeth in my way. I needed Sunbeam. Not Whitewing!

"CAWWWW!" It became an all-out war of wings.

What could I do? Whitewing wouldn't stop. The mid-air strikes and collisions caused more flapping, flipping feathers, tossing horse mane, and vulture shrieks among wind and clouds. Trying to keep his hoofs from kicking me to the moon, I dug my talons in his back, scratching deep into his hide. *Oh, my very own Whitewing! Sunbeam should have tied him up! If he only knew it was me . . .*

And for a long stretch, we twirled through the sky—me digging into his hide—until like a fierce warrior he tried to buck me off his back. *He's good. Too good,* I worried. I gripped onto his back harder. Then he flew ahead at tremendous speed, jerked and halted mid-air, sailing both of his wings out each side of his flanks to catch air. This caused a severe whiplash and shot me forward like a dart.

"CAWWWW!" *He'd done it this time! They've all done it this time!*

Seeing red, I shot toward the stars and somersaulted backwards, then circled in a large loop, swooping underneath his hoofs. I had done it! I passed him!

With him left behind, I went down for Sunbeam.

All raptor, all scavenger—I bared my teeth, pulled back my wings and dove straight toward land. My sharp bird's eye locked her in view. I aimed. The point of my beak sailed for her throat. *Wait, no! What am I—?*

I rethought for a second, but the vulture completely possessed my body. And I wasn't going down pecking for crumbs. I was diving for blood—the blood of revenge that tasted sweeter and sweeter. See, scavengers love fresh kill, no matter the source. They even eat each other. And I wasn't going hungry anymore. I would bring Sunbeam to that demon—dead or alive, freedom was mine—despite the cost.

The closer I got to my betrayer, the more vulture consumed me. Blackness enveloped my heart. A shooting black bullet, I stretched my beak wider, so my head almost split in two. Oozing with venomous anger and red with revenge, I charged, getting closer and closer to Sunbeam's throat.

"CAWWW! CAWWW!"

Suddenly—there came a flashing, white light.

The world froze. Then, complete blackness.

Long silence . . .

I came to.

What's happening? What's happening to me? I can't see. I CAN'T SEE! My head started to throb; the taste of blood filled my beak.

I'd been hit. I'd been HIT! Swiftly and out of nowhere, something had come down on top of my head.

My cord. My cord! Don't sever your cord or the door to life closes forever.

Gravely, I knew this time it wasn't the boy's flute that struck me, it was something much more powerful.

Then a voice came, "Vulture of darkness! Away with you!" the voice bellowed from the skies. I twisted my head to-and-fro, but I was still blind. It was Whitewing's voice! And the grave truth struck me: it was him. He must have struck me so hard and with such force—I didn't think I could hold on. But I was going to try. And still flapping and flying, squawking blindly, I swatted my wings at the air, until his voice rang out one last time, "I SAID, AWAY!" And he struck me with such a heavy blow, he completely snapped my great dark wing. I tumbled uncontrollably from the sky, defeated.

My cord! Don't sever your cord. Don't sever your cord.

I, the Great Wandering Scavenger, fell from the sky. And with every foot I fell from the stars, my hope for freedom fell with it.

"CAWWWW!" I wailed, but this time it sounded like a cry instead of a strong battle horn. And I dropped and twirled helplessly, my wings broken by my own beloved horse, until my head splattered into the bark of a cypress tree, and I never moved again.

CHAPTER TWENTY-NINE

GILDA

PAST
YEARS AGO

Valley of Dry Bones

I awoke with a loud cry. *Wha . . . what's happening? How long had I lain here?* It felt like I'd slept for days. I could barely move. My body ached. My face throbbed. I touched my nose and winced in pain. Dry, dark blood had crusted under my nostrils. *That must be where I hit the tree,* I thought. Breathing rapidly, I sat up.

Taking in my surroundings, I was back where I began at the start of my astral flight: the mouth of the cave. *Am I . . . am I dead?*

I raised my arm. No longer a glorious wing, but a scraped up human arm. *My* arm. I pinched myself to make sure I was alive.

My cord! My silver cord!

I remembered slamming into that cypress tree. The bird died, but my soul traveled the astral realm. I had returned to my body. To make sure, I pinched myself once more and shook my legs. Relief flooded me—as I knew for certain—my silver cord hadn't been cut. I was still alive.

Although I returned to my body, I felt more scavenger than when I'd actually been one. Sore and cut as I was, having wings made it all worth it—because for an instant—I was free. And I was fierce. Flying free as a bird and glorious through the sky, nothing could stop me. And then, the same moment I thought about me soaring, I thought about the reality of the situation. With the moon shining at the opening of the cave, my hideous scars and bruises taunted: *not yet, not free.* And a dark loneliness came over me. I shed many tears under that silver moon at the end of the cave. Beaten.

"So, do you want to punish this evil?" a voice hissed. The voice came on so suddenly I wondered how long he'd been standing there. It was Wolford. "Tell me, Gilda. Do you want to cry here like a weak lamb? Or, my little wolf, do you want revenge?" He smiled menacingly.

I turned away. "It's over. Find her yourself. I'm out." I buried my head in my hands.

"Stand up, you weakling," he scolded. "You *will* bring your betrayer to me."

I stood up. I glared at him. "No. I'm leaving. Go ahead. Do what you will. But I warn you, it'll be in your best interest not to stop me." I started to exit the cave.

"Where do you think you are going?" he said. "Finish the job!"

Suddenly, he charged me. His hand locked around my arm like an iron cuff. "Come back here. You ungrateful little wart! Pathetic lamb, you cannot defeat your own, powerful sister?" he smirked.

Something snapped inside of me. I struck Wolford across the face with such force, he shot backwards and hit the wall of the cave. A rush of energy ran down my arms and a black wind swirled violently. I levitated off the ground and raised both of my arms like wings:

"I am Gilda! I belong to no one!
You will lose, I have won!"

Everything froze. The world stopped and turned grey. The moon cast a bewitching beam in my favor. I began to see visions:

what I foresaw began to manifest. My illusions sprang to life—black fog filled the cave so thick Wolford choked and sputtered to get air. Silhouetted figures rose out from the smoke, their eyes gleaming red like phantoms.

"I am Gilda, a force you have never known!"

Before I could think or process what was happening, I shot my arms forward, the palms of my hands faced him like weapons. Wolford fell down backwards in the dirt. The whites of his eyes rolled desperately in the fog.

"Gilda! Halt! I will kill you if you ruin this! Pull back, Gilda. Pull back!" he warned in an icy rage. In the next moment, he vaporized in the smoke. There was nothing left of him until with the help of some dark magic, his cold, blue eyes glared at me from a thousand directions in the cave. His voice echoed and boomed throughout the chamber: "Where are you going? No one else wants you. Not even your own flesh and blood!"

I raised my arms and levitated higher—higher. The wind picked up and grew darker. "Be gone! You will lose. I have won!" I chanted, resisting his wicked sorcery. And this collision of black magic collided in the walls of the cave for a long while until . . .

Wolford's voice boomed from the bottom of some abyss:

"Betrayed by your blood,
Left for dead,
Your future is mine,
In Sheol and dread!
Sleep fall upon you
Like the darkness of dead!"

Then something inside me cracked and drained. My arms grew heavy, and I started to tremble. I felt seconds from fainting and sleepy. Exhaustion lowered my eyelids. My dark, violent wind was fading. I hit the ground hard, no longer levitating, but on foot. *I'm losing power,* I thought. Then to my horror, his hexing fangs, growling at me from a thousand directions, became a beehive of swarming daggers in the chamber, all swiping over me, until the swarm of a thousand bloody blades melded into two glaring eyes—and his face materialized before me. And he, standing less than an inch away, leaned in and hissed, "Betrayed by your own beloved. Who else wants you?" Then his whole body materialized, and he struck me brutally across the face. A light flashed. I lost my footing and collapsed.

He bent down and pulled me up. Trying to stand, I wobbled at the knees. He tightened his grasp on my arm. "Your powers are becoming evident," he hissed in my ear and smiled savagely. "That's the little wolf inside of you. Remember, I am the leader of the pack since the very beginning. Now, apologize."

"That will be a cold day in hell." I stammered.

He grabbed a fistful of my hair and squeezed. He dragged me all the way down the mazy halls of the catacomb. "Time for you to go back home." He shoved me to the ground and picked up a large chain, larger than the one before. One by one, he locked each bolt on it. I bit my lip to keep from crying. I'd never let him see me cry.

"Good, little girl." Before leaving, he dropped a large cup of elixir, and slammed down the ancient *Book of Shadows* next to my chains. "Drink, child."

"I hate you," I replied.

He smiled threateningly and walked out.

In my chains, I felt the scavenger grow. I had to nurture that feeling. Why? It was the only moment I felt alive. I took a big gulp of the elixir. I closed my eyes, and although caged, in my mind I was flying. I soared over Sunbeam and Whitewing, and Father and all their faces—until the drug took effect, and I lay down in my chains, free as a dark, glorious winged raptor.

I hate you. I hate you all.

CHAPTER THIRTY

PRESENT
13 YEARS OLD

Holding cell, Realm of the Dark Night

The stone's green glow glints through my half-open eyelids. I awake from my past, back to the present. *I must sort these memories.* Serpentine, reliably on my neck, sucks the eerie afterglow back into itself. I clutch my stone and sit up. A tear escapes my eye, splashing on the ground. And I realize I must have looked at the ground a whole minute, shedding tears.

Suddenly, I spot the plant. I dry my eyes and lean in to examine it. *How strange.* The little plant in the corner of my cell, it's grown another sprout. The veins on the bud curl like intricate calligraphy, forming another peculiar word:

εΐσοδος ταχέως

What's it mean? Hmm. I know the first leaf reads *I AM.* I ponder what this second word could mean. I analyze it, running my finger over the leaf's silky texture, muttering, "I am . . . I am . . . I AM—WHAT?"

Suddenly, in the instant I say "I AM" aloud, the fresh garden breeze comes into the cell. The veins on the leaf pulse gold, shimmering and spiraling to reveal the cryptic words in my own language until they read:

COMING SOON

My stone leaps on my chest. *What on earth? Serpentine knows something.* Then a gold mist fills my prison, cool and fragrant like flowers. It swirls and glimmers rosy gold. Then a white light flashes bright as the sun. I shut my eyes to block the gleam. When I open them, standing in my cell, is the Quiet Gardener. He's already watering the little plant. He's dressed in a white tunic with a sash of spring colors, all the way down to his sandals. I stare, speechless. Then he turns and gazes directly at me. "Daughter, what kind of pain must you feel to let this fire consume your heart," he says.

Although I'd just been shedding tears alone, seeing him lifts my heart. His dazzling, brown eyes sparkle. He looks very joyful to see me. And I feel like I've always known him.

"My child, do not be afraid. Do not lose hope."

He sits down next to me. Seeing my cuts and bruises, his countenance becomes serious. "Daughter, I know you have little strength. Eat." He pulls ripe, colorful fruit from a basket: apples, figs, pomegranate, sweet oranges, and that bread. The most delicious, sweet bread. "Now, how are you getting along, my daughter?" he asks.

"I want out. I can't take this anymore. I might as well die!"

"Hold on a little while longer, Gilda. Your hour of trial is coming to an end."

I don't realize my hunger until I put the bread in my mouth. Between mouthfuls, I ask, "I don't understand. What is ending? And what's coming soon? I need out of here. I have wolves to kill, evil to punish!"

As if knowing my thoughts, he says, "My child, you believe only wolves can defeat wolves? Only evil defeats evil?"

"I know it," I say, between a bite of tasty fig.

"Daughter, you say, 'I seek revenge! I punish wolves like a wolf! I do not need help!' Child, you do not realize this makes you pitiful and blind."

"Blind? What?" I snap. "You do not know what I've suffered. You know nothing!" I throw down the fig. Oddly, the fig withers on the ground and shrivels. *Wha . . . What is—?*

"Child, I have known you since the beginning." He smiles. "I am here now, eating with you." He stands and lifts his tunic to reveal a deep scar on his side.

"How did you get that scar?" I reach to touch his side. An electric pulse shoots down my arm. I feel power in him. Peace warms my heart.

"I am the Lamb, pierced for all. Gentle and meek, but mightier than many wolves. Do not repay evil for evil, lest you become like the wolves you seek to slay."

"Are you a king?" I ask. Although not dressed as a king, he moves and speaks like one.

"Daughter, my kingdom is not here, but I fill the whole universe with myself. Hear my voice. I know betrayal. I know suffering." He gazes at me. "But take heart, you can conquer it."

"A king? Why would you waste your time here—on me—in some dark, forgotten cell?"

"I take care of all that has been given to me. I tend and prune everything that is in my care. I bring light in your darkness, but you have not understood it. Take heart, I am coming soon."

"Where? Coming where?" I stare at his magnetic eyes. Gazing into mine, he evokes deep emotions. He seems to know me and all the unfairness I've suffered. And it makes me want to cry, but not a bad cry, a good kind of cry. A feeling of warm light and air washes my heart.

Suddenly, the little plant in the corner gleams and grows taller. I freeze. I feel hypnotized, but calm and peaceful, and then a glimmer of hope makes my heart flutter. And before my eyes, the reddest, ripest fruit blooms on the stem! Then comes his soothing voice like a bubbling brook:

"Gilda, in your time of suffering, I counsel you to eat my fruit, so your tainted gown can become white to wear, and cover all your darkness. And all your troubles will become long forgotten, like waters that have passed by."

"I don't understand." As he speaks, none of it makes much sense to my mind, but somehow, his words resonate inside of me. I'm seeing in a new sort of way: as with the eyes of my heart.

"Child, do not eat the bitterness of your own food. But of the branch, and the fruit that will bring you joy." He walks to the plant and smears a streak of red sap from the plant. It gleams and drips down his finger like blood. "This blood-sap will wash away all your gloominess. The fire in you, instead of burning you up, will refine you like gold. In your pain of betrayal, my tree will be a canopy over you, a shelter and shade from the heat of your anger, a refuge and healing place from your storms and rain."

"How can I get this? How will I know what to do?"

"I counsel you to listen to my voice, so you can hear—and this blood-red salve, on your eyes, so you can see." The salve drips like blood. "This is not the blood of vengeance, but of mercy. I offer it freely, but you bear the weight of opening your eyes."

I can't speak anymore, for too many things have been said. I sit in silence, pondering many things in my heart.

In the next moment, the fresh garden wind comes and begins to swirl—swirl—SWIRL—into a beautiful golden mist. With the wind loud and blasting, the Gardener begins to vaporize inside of it. "Child, do what is right," he warns in the cool wind, slowly fading "for evil lurks at your door. It desires to take you, but you must rule over it. I've come to tell you they are wicked and demonic. They are murderers from the beginning, seeking to destroy. They have no regard for love."

"No! Wait! Don't leave! How will I defeat it?"

"You must wake up, so you can see. I am with you. Listen to my voice," he says in the sheen of fading glory. "FOR I AM COMING SOON!" And as quickly as he'd come, in a flash, he is gone.

CHAPTER THIRTY-ONE

LORD WOLFORD

PRESENT

My Dear Abaddon,

I note with grave severity that He, our great enemy, has entered the darkness of Gilda's holding cell. It is urgent. He has come.

You must not make light of this dire situation. We are running out of time. But, my boy, do not despair. Some believers have returned home to our realm after a brief encounter in His presence. For they are slaves to their own calamity.

Gilda's abominations are not simple for her to cast aside. She is weak and overrun by heavy darkness, by things in her past too shocking to say aloud. At present, she gropes in the dark, feeling her way through the red walls of revenge—hoping to find light.

Keep her in this haze. Double down! Never let the truth come to the surface. For once it does, she will escape her cell, and will not be easily managed. In fact, she will become a powerful force, dangerous to our realm.

We are at the pivotal hour. We still have time: for my boy—she still cannot hear, nor can she clearly see.

Your Prince,

LORD WOLFORD

CHAPTER THIRTY-TWO

GILDA

PRESENT
13 YEARS OLD

Holding cell, Realm of the Dark Night

"Now," I urge my stone. "Help me escape, or I'll be stuck here forever while everyone else's life goes on." I clutch Serpentine, my hands smeared with dirt.

Open your eyes, so you can see, the Gardener's words stick. Blood has dripped down the branch. Dry, red sap has hardened into teardrops on the stem.

I am a seer. Why would the Gardener say I can't see? There is supreme power in him. I sense it. But how could I be wrong? I belong to no one. Surely, my powers will light the path of escape.

"Miss Gilda, I have your elixir." It's Abaddon.

Funny, I haven't had any since the Gardener came. Haven't thought of my elixir since I ate his delicious bread and drank his sparkling water.

"Come in," I blurt.

He opens the door, holding the candle that burns a blue flame. Strangely, it burns warmer tonight. Not as cold and blue, but sort of a softer, golden flame.

"Your candle flame, it looks—" I mutter.

"My flame? What color does it look now?" His tone sounds interrogating.

"Oh, I don't know . . . sort of golden."

"I see. Well, your drink, miss," he hands me the cup. I turn away. "Miss Gilda, your drink?"

"Set it down. I'll get to it later."

He studies me with his black eyes. The blue flame reflects in his stare. A sense of uneasiness shoots down my spine. *His presence is different from the Gardener's. His brought calmness. Abaddon's brings the restless swarm of butterflies.*

He turns away and sets the candle in the sconce on the iron wall. It flickers dimly in the cell. He has a wildness about him as he walks toward me. "Is everything OK?" He touches the small of my back and pulls me toward him.

"Abaddon, where am I?" Suddenly, I sense he knows more than he lets on, deep secrets in those black orbs.

"I told you, Gilda. I know as much as you." He leans in to embrace me. "Sensing your anguish this close is a bit overwhelming." He lowers his hands to the curve of my hips. He sways me, playfully slow dancing.

"You seem upset. Let's dance." Although he moves in elegance, like an aristocratic, highborn dancer, I sense something roguish in his smile. The cut of his V-neck reveals the ink-mark across his chest.

Something feels different. In step with him, I know I'm in a realm between the living and the dead. That much I have recently realized because the light is much dimmer than the living world, but not entirely snuffed out. Just grey, dull, and lifeless. Up close, my eyes study the mark across his chest: **καταστρέφω**.

Suddenly, a sense of urgency rises in my stomach. *You're in the final hour. Child, do what is right. Sin is lurking at your door,* comes the Gardener's voice.

"Gilda, is something wrong?"

"I told you, I'm fine." I glance at the leaf. The blood-sap has seeped into the leaves' veins as if giving it life: the veins gleam red against the green springtime petals. *Beautiful.*

"It's that plant!" he snaps. "I'm afraid it's poisonous. That blood! It's sick. Don't get close to it." He turns away. I feel him slightly tremble; he shudders at the sight of the blood on the branch. He can barely look at it. "I sent word for its removal. This weed is dangerous."

"I told you. I don't want it removed!"

"What do you mean?" He frowns. "I could sense it the instant I entered your cell, Gilda. Don't you trust me? Here, drink." He picks up the chalice and puts it to my lips.

More elixir, misssss? Like you, I too, have lived hidden among rocks alone. I will always be with you. We are familiar. Vengy's memory suddenly flashes before me as Abaddon holds the elixir to my lips. *I've been here before.* I begin seeing the old in the present moment, connecting pieces together. But why? My heart begins to race. What is happening? *Open your eyes, so you can see.* The Gardener's words resonate louder.

"I don't want it. Not right now."

"I see," he stares off for a second, lost in thought. He sets the drug down on the floor of my cell, near my mat. "Well, since we're being so honest and pure as snow, let me take you to heaven." He picks me up playfully and twirls me. Holding me, he leans in to give me a kiss. This time, the unworldly feeling we'd shared now feels distant: dull, lifeless, and draining.

"Put me down," I say.

"What's the matter with you?" He sets me on foot, gazing at me. "You should know this attitude only makes me want to be with you more. And you should know before the night is over, I will."

"Stop, Abaddon." I turn away. My heart pounds intermixed with both alarm and repulsion.

"I'm not letting you go. I've decided I'm going to help you get out of here—and we're going to end those traitors. Look what they've done to you." He smiles demurely then backs me to the wall. Flirtatiously, he wrestles around and pins me to the ground. Now on the ground, he grabs the elixir again. "Gilda, you can feel free. Get free . . . feel free." He tips the cup to my mouth. The smell of it, like crushed leaf and gasoline, fills my nose. My heart pounds harder than ever. Oh, I do want my drug. He shoves the rim of the cup between my lips. I drink. It trickles down my throat. I slowly lose control. My senses detach—again—I'm floating—in that cloud that once brought relief but now seems like a blur of beautiful doom.

"See, now you can stop being so cold."

Still on the ground, we're lying side by side, our bodies close to each other. He pulls my body into his. "I want us close. Let it be right now." In the flicker of the flame, he's mostly shadows. Before I know it. He pins me on my back.

"Abaddon, stop! What's wrong with you?" I push him away. He sits up laughing.

"Gilda, I'm only teasing! Where is your sense of fun?" he says. He dips his finger in the drug, dripping, and shoves it into my mouth. He wrestles me to the ground again and snakes his hand under my back and pulls my body tightly into his; then runs his hand down my stomach. "You are mine. We belong together." His voice is raspy, pulling my head closer to try and kiss me.

Alarming danger surges through me. "What the hell's wrong with you? You need to GO!" I push him off and jump to my feet.

"Go?" he smirks. He stands up and leans toward me, thumbing Serpentine. "You know, this stone is hard and cold, just like you."

Only a night ago, we had talked and laughed for hours. I'd never felt so close to anyone in my life. That is the effect he had on me. Never in a hundred years did I imagine myself the type: completely overrun with the thrill of someone's attention. He made me feel so adored, so comfortable, like I'd always known him. But now, he feels estranged: like we'd known each other for a moment, but that moment's gone, and we're drifting apart.

"I want to be alone," I say.

He starts to hand me the cup. "Here, have more drink."

"I don't want it!" *What am I thinking? Why don't I want it?*

"Gilda, calm down."

He starts to hold it under my nose. Before I can think, I swipe the air, knocking it from his hand. The cup shatters on the cell floor. "I'm going to tell you, Abaddon—I can't be tamed!" I blurt before I know what I'm saying.

He stares at me, his eyebrows raised in shock. Then he smiles, roguishly. "Angry, are you? Kisssss me. I'm hungryyyy. Kisss meeee." He backs me against the wall and playfully bites my lip. My blood drips down his chin. His eyes turn wild.

Don't ever bite me again, Vengy! I recall.

"Oh, you're so dangerousssss," Abaddon mocks.

"What the hell are you doing? STOP! It would be in your best interest to leave—NOW!"

Something changes in his dark eyes, and he grabs me and squeezes tighter and tighter until I'm trying to break free, and everything is going black, as black as his eyes. He grimaces, "I didn't know this place was a whorish den of abomination."

"WHAT? Get off me, you stupid bastard!"

I try to push him off, wriggling my arms inside his bear grip with my back against the wall. My legs somewhat free, I'm kicking him in the shins. This scuffle causes me to knock against the little plant. We fall to the ground. A drop of the plant's blood-salve splashes on my skin—and suddenly—the world freezes. Everything stops. And what comes next leaves me speechless. Something like black snake scales fall off my eyelids. *What on earth?* A bright light flashes. The black scales shimmer pearlescent in a pulse of light then whirl into a golden mist. All my senses heighten—a vision manifests—and with

Abaddon's black orbs frozen, staring into mine, I begin to see way deep down into those black, bottomless eyes:

❧ ❧

I see that long ago, a gigantic red creature with the face of a wolf and the tail of a dragon had been hurled to the earth. As it fell, the red dragon-wolf bared a name on its tail, but the name was secret and one I am forbidden to mention aloud.

The red wolf was blowing blue flames from its mouth, blue flames filled with icy rage and cold loneliness as it was hurled into darkness by the High King—known as the God of Lights. The further down the wolf fell, the more the voice of God pealed across the skies like lightning, "This accuser and destroyer of mankind has been cast down! But mankind will triumph over him—by the blood of my Lamb! For I AM COMING SOON!"

The red dragon-wolf scoffed at the God of Lights, falling down—down—down—until it dropped into a deep abyss: a pit as dark and bottomless as Abaddon's eyes. Then the red wolf came out of the abyss and waged war against earth, shouting: "Woe to the earth and to the seas! Because I, the destroyer, have come down to it! Mankind's lives will be short, painful, and bitter, just as my life has become!"

Then the wolf roared, and unbelievably, what came next was completely true. It started to shapeshift with a long, agonizing growl while its sharp, bloody fangs shrunk; its pointy ears flattened into human ears, and its scaly body was covered with flesh until its hairy face smoothed into a mask of a fine, eloquent man, and that man—to my horror—bore the face of Lord Wolford—a hideous, masquerading demon. He vowed, "My revenge is on Him who is most high! I will have your throne, Oh God of Lights! It is mine!"

And as he stood at the shaft of the abyss, smoke rose from it like the smoke from an enormous underworld. The smoke rose and rose until it darkened the sun.

"This is the first woe; many other woes are to come!" he roared. He raised his fist and screamed at the sky. "My revenge will find you, oh King of Kings! And though I cannot destroy you, I'll destroy all that you love—and entice mankind—your most precious beloveds—into this abyss of torment where you have cast me!"

And the God of Light responded. His voice boomed so loud it shook the earth, "I, the God of Light, have cast you down for your pride. You have willed destruction in your heart and chosen darkness for light." Then it poured down rain because the God of Lights wept and wept for the earth.

Then to my horror, Lord Wolford, that devil, was holding a giant key to the hatch of the abyss. Wolford stood tall, like an angel of light with his blonde hair and sparkling blue eyes. He shouted, "Destroyer! Come forth!" and to my shock, an inanimate thing slithered up from the ground to Wolford's feet then shapeshifted into a man—it was Abaddon!

Wolford turned to Abaddon and said, "Oh loyal one, you have chosen to fall with me and my legion of dark angels. Do you consent, at this hour, to wage war against our enemy, the God of Lights, and for me to cut and mark you as my very own?"

"I do," Abaddon smirked at the sky.

And swelling with pride, Wolford raised his claw into the air. It glinted red like hot iron, and to Abaddon, he gloated, "You shall be called—Angel of the Abyss!" Then he brought down his claw, searing the mark—καταστρέφω—across Abaddon's chest.

That name! The one I'd seen on Abaddon's chest! He's one of them! The name started to scramble in a whirl of black snake scales, the scales that had fallen off my eyes, keeping me blind, until they all vanished, and I understood the name in my own language, which read—DESTROYER.

I was shaking and utterly horrified and screamed, "What do you want? Why me? Leave me alone! Why must I see this?" And to my utter shock, Abaddon shrank down and shapeshifted into many forbidden abominations until he was slithering on the ground as Vengy! VENGY? OH VENGEANCE! MY FAMILIAR!

Suddenly—

Before my eyes came my little plant, which started to sprout and bear colorful fruit until it grew into a beautiful, gigantic tree. Marveling at it, suddenly, the God of Light's voice spoke to me, "Daughter, do not be afraid of the wolves. From my tree I give life, and every leaf is for healing. I have sent my son to tend and prune it, so you can find rest in my shade. Be healed from your wounds and receive joy for every tear."

And suddenly, a pack of wolves gathered behind Wolford with Vengeance, my own snake, wrapped around his smooth neck. Then Wolford turned to me and snarled. His legion bared bloody fangs and started toward me to devour me, until I heard the God of Light's voice thunder across the whole earth, "I AM THE LAMB, MIGHTIER THAN WOLVES! DO NOT TOUCH MY BELOVED!" And they dropped to the ground and crawled backward on all fours like whipped dogs. Then a warm light like springtime shined on my face, and tremendous strength charged down my body.

And the Gardener's voice resonated like refreshing waters through me: "Daughter, open your eyes, so you can see."

And I woke up.

❧ ☙

The vision collapses. The mist fades. Snapping back, everything resumes. I'm back where I left off, flat on my back, weak and swooning underneath Abaddon's strong grip. He's still glaring down at me, but everything is quite clear. *He's one of them. Vengy? My own shapeshifter who helped me catch lawbreakers is now trying to catch me? Oh, no! My own familiar! After all we'd been through, he's now out for my blood!*

"What have you seen?" he growls. "Has someone been in here? It's that old weed! That's what it is!" He grabs a ball of my hair and pulls it so hard I feel dizzy. "Telling me to leave? Who else would want you, tainted as you are?"

Who else would want you? Wolford's face flashes. *No one wants you, not even your own flesh and blood,* his words haunt me.

"Vengy? You? How could you?" *Another betrayal.*

"No, missssss, you betrayed me! You left me in the pit!" he hissed. "You promised to feed me then abandoned me like an old rag. Lawbreaker!"

"Oh, Vengy! But shapeshifting on *me*, your own familiar? Such awful, wicked sorcery!" My heart sinks. My body weakens.

Then, to my utter shock, Abaddon strikes me hard across the face. "Look at you! All your abominations. You deserve hell! You promised to feed me and keep me alive. The blood of vengeance is a glorious, terrifying thing. Oh, I'm sssooo hungry!"

For a moment, gazing into his eyes, I understand his pain, his rage, and our deep connection softens me to him.

"We were familiar, Gilda. We were so familiar. And we still are," he says, gripping me tighter and tighter with my blood dripping down his chin. "You belong in the underworld! Punish their evil! You belong with us, in the pit! Serve or die!" He's squeezing me so hard I'm about to faint.

Suddenly, at the thought of being back in that demon's pit, I tense. Something snaps inside of me. My powers begin to rise.

"I am Gilda, you will learn who I am!" I strike Abaddon in the chest. He flies backward. I get to my feet and raise my arms like wings:

"Serpentine, I calleth thee,
in the hour of darkness,
devour the snake,
set me FREE!"

Abaddon staggers to his feet and lunges at me. I come down hard, striking him across the face, sending him soaring. He splats against the iron wall.

"I am Gilda, I belong to no one!" my voice reverberates, filling the whole cell. Then comes a black rush of wind. I start my levitation—and clutch Serpentine:

"Stone of vengeance,
no one can break,
strike this beast
with Serpentine and snakes!"

Serpentine casts her eerie glow, which morphs into green shapes like snakes, twisting and striking, scattering into a thousand moving flecks, descending upon Abaddon. They strike him hard, mercilessly.

"Gilda! Stop! Please, Gilda!" he swats uselessly, a crease of terror stretches across his wide-eyed face.

In the next second, Abaddon shapeshifts into a snake, becoming Vengy in my cloud of black smoke. "Ssssss!" he hisses then vanishes. His voice comes from somewhere in the cell. "Come with me. Back home. To hell you belong! Punish evil! Sssslay your traitorssss!" Shadowy, moving masses rise from the ground like locusts, streaking across my vision. *Wha . . . what's happening . . .* ?

In a flash, Abaddon materializes an inch from my face, as a man again, in a black- hooded robe, snarling through his fangs. "By the time I'm done with you, you'll wish for death," he whispers. "You'll wish for death, you fool, but you'll get only more torture for your sins!"

"You bastard! You lied to me!" I slam my arm down to strike him, but he grabs and locks onto my wrist like a metal cuff.

"Yes, but you accepted them." He grins. "Why? Because you wanted every one of those lies. With your drug and abominations and your cold black heart—hard as that green stone you wear—like a noose around your neck! And so, you'll be hung from it!"

Then to my horror, he draws a large onyx sword. He points the blade of it toward my chest. "Legion—SSSTRIKE!" He hisses. Suddenly, the black locusts, which had been hovering behind him, come in a loud rush, swarming all over me. They sting with the power of red scorpions: my face, arms, legs, consuming every inch of exposed flesh. "A sting for every sin!" he accuses. "You are a disgrace! A killer. A Lawbreaker. Come home, little wolf. Destroy them, as they have destroyed you!"

"Abaddon, I'm warning you—cease!" I'm still on my feet. I feel faint but at the same time, strength starts to resurge inside of me.

"Come home! To hell you belong!"

Amid the panic, I'm dizzy and holding on, but my strength rises and rises. "I'm warning you Abaddon—I cannot be tamed!"

Abaddon answers with a laugh:

"Oh, Vengeance,
bound at the chasm of the pit,
release the plague of poison,
Tear her bit by bit!"

And with his dark sorcery, the locusts emit a pillar of thick, putrid fog until I'm coughing and gasping for air.

"Abaddon! Stop!" I warn between breaths, until the fog finally dissipates. And with the fog cleared from my eyes, I look up to find something terrible: the locusts still swarm on me, but they look changed, for their faces have morphed, resembling human faces—the faces of my betrayers. They fly through me like ghosts.

I gasp and drop from levitating. Staggering on my feet, I feel as though something carries me off, and the memories rush through me, so lifelike, that I swear I'm reliving each one of them.

In the mix of this horror, Abaddon's ears start to point upward. His flesh stretches and peels back until his mask falls and shatters on the prison floor, revealing a forked tongue and scales all over his grotesque reptilian face—the face of Vengy, my familiar, more hideous than I ever saw Vengeance look before. "Do not end her," he growls to the locusts. "But strike her with agony. She will long for death, but death will not find her." He studies my face.

It is urgent. My heart hammers. I feel an odd, squeezing sensation, like someone's trying to squeeze and search out all my weaknesses. My betrayers swarm, stinging me as locusts again and again, shooting through me until the memories whirl into a great black storm—whirling and rising—until—suddenly—I BREAK. Darkness envelops me.

In a burst, I push pack. My eyes glow, casting sharp beams and lighting the cell green. My palms flash out in front of me, slamming Abaddon against the cell wall. The raptor commences—my wings materialize and stretch across the cell—all scavenger. I command Serpentine:

"Stone of power,
no one can break
strike this beast
with Serpentine and snakes!"

I stretch out my arms like wings. *I will be free.* My shadow on the wall moves when I move, and when I swoop my arms, they are two, terrifying raptor wings that fill the whole prison cell. I transform. All scavenger. Sorcery levitates me. "I am Gilda. I belong to no one!" My voice booms like a mighty fowl, a great battle horn.

Abaddon holds his hands up to his face. He flinches back. “Gilda! Wait!” he begs.

But it’s too late. The vulture has possessed me. *He will die here today.*

“Stone of power,
no one can break,
swallow this beast,
with Serpentine and snakes!”

My stone flashes and sets off a slimy, green glow. A violent, irresistible wave of ice and heat pulse through me. My eyes burn hot and radiate; the entire cell glares witchy green. *Murder in the name of righteousness. Only wolves defeat wolves.* Uncontrollable darkness rises inside of me. I tremble uncontrollably and ache for him to pay—for *all* of them to pay.

“Strike this lying beast,
with Serpentine and Snakes!”

The darkness bows down to me. My stone casts thousands of glowing green snakes that pour down in droves like a rainstorm. They hiss and stretch their mouths wide open, swallowing up Abaddon’s locusts until they’re all devoured.

“Gilda, please!” Abaddon shrinks back, baring his teeth, but this time in terror. I absorb the wickedness inside of him, absorb every one of those memories and all my evil betrayers—until I lose complete control.

As I glare into his black eyes, he falls down shuddering, “No! Don’t do it!”

“I am Gilda! You will learn who I am!
And you will NEVER return through this port,
For I, Gilda, now cut forever,

your SILVER CORD!"

Then I raise my sharp wing, all scavenger—all vulture—and bring it down on him in one hard blow, with the force of a mighty battleax. He collapses, face down in the dirt of the cell—completely limp—and vaporizes in a whirlwind of smoke and ash. And his candle that burns a blue flame on the sconce, snuffs out in one icy blow.

He is gone.

Exhausted, I fall from levitating. I drop down on foot, catching my breath, for much energy has been drained.

A tear escapes my eye and splashes in the dirt. *For a second, I really thought he . . . Abaddon . . . Vengy? I should have known. Trust no one . . .* that's been my life mantra, a cesspool of deceit and shattered love. I snap to. *Stand up on your feet, little wolf.* In the same moment, I'm embarrassed of my own behavior—crying over some lying snake. I raise my chest like armor made of steel. I clutch my fist. *I am Gilda. I belong to no one.*

When the fog from the sorcery clears, lo and behold! There lies—can it be?—Abaddon's key! The key to my cell! Right here on the prison floor! My heart thumps with tremendous relief. I wipe my eyes. I have done it! Wolves do defeat wolves!

"I'm free? I am! I can't believe it! I AM FREE! SERPENTINE, YOU DID IT. WE ARE FREE! Now I will slay the rest of those wolves!"

I scoop up the key and run to the door, twist it, but the door remains locked. "Locked?" I pant. "Open! Open you old thing!" I pull and twist and kick, but the iron door doesn't budge. It's sealed completely shut. And I know that even the darkest magic of all will not open it.

I collapse on the prison floor. I bury my head in my hands with nothing but plans to get even. Nothing but fury to my right, and angst to my left as companions. "What? How? It's not fair!" I scream—red with rage—until the Gardener's words thunder inside me:

Open your eyes, so you can see.

CHAPTER THIRTY-THREE

LORD WOLFORD

PRESENT

Dear Abaddon,

I watch with great disappointment at your failure. I should run a dagger through your worthless body for your pathetic attempt as General Destroyer, Angel of the Abyss. I have ordered a ring of guards around your cage. You are banished under lock and key, for she has cut your silver cord. You will remain at the bottom of the abyss, to wallow in your failure, and for the disgrace to the Valley of Dry Bones, our entire underworld. But, my boy, you will be all the wiser for it.

Powerful as you are, dare I wonder if you caught affection for the girl? If so, this consequence is what even a tiny shred of love will do. Destroyer: you bear that name to destroy weakness, not let it destroy you. My boy, you cannot really love. Nobody can. Always decide against it.

You will find that if you search any human heart, they are haunted by painful memories they once called love—some much worse than others. Weak lambs! This darkens their intellect. Gilda's intellect is more ill-tempered than before. It is urgent. Now is the time, for her last attempt at love has never before so easily thrown her into the passion of explosive revenge. Everything has been taken from her.

I must go. We are in the final hour. Your task is over. You have failed. Because of your failure, I will go to Gilda—myself.

Watch and learn how the pain of shattered love kills the weak, and anger slays the simple. The final hour draws near. This is her last chance, and the chance I ensure, that she stays blind. Hold on, my boy. I am bringing her back home.

Your Prince,

Lord Wolford

CHAPTER THIRTY-FOUR

PRESENT
13 YEARS OLD

Holding cell, Realm of the Dark Night

It is the last hour. I know this for sure because I sense it. The weight of time pushes down on me. I've been locked in here nine whole months. Knowing this is my last night, I pull at the prison door. "Open! Open you damn thing! You infect my eyes!" I kick and pull it, casting the fiercest hexes of magic.

Nothing. It's sealed completely shut.

Rage courses through my veins. I want my elixir—but realize I hadn't had a drop since I slayed Abaddon. He won't be returning with it, that's for sure. So, I preserve the one last cup of it I have left for when I start violent withdrawals. It sits next to my mat for safe keeping.

Thinking of him, a tear escapes my eye and splashes in the dirt. What a deceitful, conniving, grotesque character. In hindsight, I see so many things that are repulsive about him. I don't know how I ever trusted him. If I even did truly care for him at all! Next time, I won't be so gullible. But there won't ever be a next time—ever, ever, ever! There are so many things I'd like to say to him.

I push all our moments to the back of my mind. There's no time for regrets or wallowing. He deserves what he got. With the elixir almost gone and leaving my bloodstream, all the memories I long to forget flood through me. No more escaping with my drug. I have to face everything, feel it all. *NOOO!*

In a second of despair, I rip my stone from my chest and throw it on the floor. "You're worthless! Serpentine, you've failed! You're a disgrace! Here I am—still locked up! With only one last gulp of elixir!" Then I commence to kicking my own crystal. I hate it! It rolls and clangs on the ground, but doesn't break, remaining hardened.

Long silence.

"I'm sorry." I pick up Serpentine. "I'm so sorry. You're the only solid thing I have left." I pet Serpentine and wipe off the smudges; then hang it back around my neck. "Time is running out. I cannot break."

My heart beats wildly. I study the little plant, which now has riper fruit and red blood-salve covering the entire stem. Desperation opens my mouth. I mutter, "God, if you're out there, help me see."

In the next moment, ever so subtly, I hear a voice—a voice I like best of all—calling my name. I sense I've heard it before, but from where? *Maybe I'm just overly tired.* "Gilda," comes the voice again. I dart my eyes around the cell, lest there be any more imposters. My eyes study my plant. The leaves subtly start to move, but there's no breeze. My hearts thumps wildly. I walk closer toward it. Suddenly, a rustling fills the cell, like a forest of trees blowing in the wind. The wind carries a haunting song yet croons the most beautiful chorus I've ever heard.

Awe-struck, I cannot turn away from the plant. I stare, hypnotized. The more I gaze at it my heart lifts, feeling like a ray of spring sun. And the more the wind blows, the louder the celestial music fills my ears. As the little plant begins to gust in the whirl of the spring breeze, it no longer looks like a little plant, but spreads out and grows branches with so much foliage it looks like a leafy, shaggy beard—and then—looks like the face of a man. Although I should feel terrified, I'm not. For I have seen this face before. It's *him*—the Quiet Gardner, the man of light.

Then his voice flows through the cell like a rushing waterfall, "Daughter, my tree is life and every leaf, for your healing." Then a bright light, like the sun, glares from the mystical tree.

I clutch Serpentine. "Show me!" She casts her eerie glow, but it pales in comparison to the tree's bright, white light.

Then I feel as if someone touches my shoulder. *It's happening, another vision*. I brace myself, the vision casts me backwards—knowing this will be the very last time I'm thrust into the nightmare I long to forget but cannot escape. And as I'm thrust into it—the Gardener's words echo, "I will counsel you: listen to my voice so you can hear, and open your eyes, so you can see.

THE END OF THE BEGINNING

GILDA

PAST
13 YEARS OLD

Valley of Dry Bones

I had been here before, nine months earlier, in Wolford's cave. Sunbeam had come to make it all right. But it was too late. Besides, after all she'd done, could I trust her?

Like waves, the risk of the wrong decision swept over me in heavy blows and breakers, intermixed with fears that kept me frozen, but to not act at all was more terrifying than ever.

Forced to do the *hard* thing, the only way out was . . . to kill my *beloved.*

❧ ❧

I left Wolford in the chamber. His offer still stood: *End Sunbeam, and you can go free.* Hours had gone by as I quietly, ever so quietly, made my way to find Sunbeam in the vast pit, secretly treading through the maze of the corridor. I'd made up my mind to end her life. Rid myself of her forever. I just needed to find her. Finding her in the pit was not without challenge, but anything in life worth doing doesn't come without a challenge, right?

I crept through endless stone covens of sorcery and catacombs. I would get justice. I would get free. Now before you think I'm mad, you know nothing of what I endured: the hundreds of injuries I tolerated. I did the best I could until Sunbeam's final deceits threatened my own life. She'd gone too far. Vengeance was mine. The final hour had come. She'd be punished—feel the impact—in the same impact she'd injured me. Do not think of me, even once, as insane. See, insanity drives people to punish others without cause. I, on the other hand, had justified reasons. I suffered unfairly at her game. Any reasonable, self-dignified person would stand up for themselves for such evil committed against them. And oh! You should have seen how brilliantly I proceeded.

I continued forward for about fifty paces until—finally!—I sensed her close—closer—so close my heart began to pound out of my chest. And I stood still in the darkness, composing myself in the excitement and nearness of her proximity. I had to be extremely cautious. If she had the slightest notion I was nearby, or that I would harm her, she could fly upon me. But I was prepared: my dark magic an equal match to her powers. *Your freedom is near,* Wolford's voice urged me on. I preceded with caution down the stone passageway. Being a seer, my senses heightened, sensing her precise location.

About twenty more paces down the narrow hall, I rounded the corner with great trepidation. Carefully, so carefully, I peeked only my head around the stone to get a clearer view, not to alarm her to my presence. And . . . and peeking my keen eye around the bend . . . I saw her! My pulse quickened. It was like seeing a ghost, except only it wasn't a ghost from time's past, it was really Sunbeam. I watched her. She was unaware of my presence. And it took me a long time to get the rest of my body, secretly, into the aperture where she stood. And then what came next appalled me. For Whitewing stood right beside her. *Oh! Not again! She should have tied him up this time!*

I could barely contain my feelings. I was minutes from freedom. Glory was near! Cautiously, ever so cautiously, moving in the slowest of motion, I crept up behind her. It was black as night in the stone chamber. My heart hammered so loudly in my chest, she must have felt it because she whipped her neck to the side and panted, "Who's there? Show yourself!"

My movements, subtle as they were, jolted to a complete stop. Not even the tiniest twitch escaped from me. I stood completely still, barely breathing, still as a statue. When I had patiently waited long enough, I continued forward. Closer—stealthily—so quiet I crept until I was standing only an inch behind her. Overcome with excitement, I secretly grinned behind her at the expense of her punishment.

"Gilda?" she whispered, as if sensing my presence. But little did she know her attempts to salvage our togetherness were all in vain. For *death* was now upon her, about to make her a victim—as she had made me for five long years.

Long silence. Heartbeat—THUMP THUMP—THUMP THUMP.

Staring ahead at the walls of her doom, she must have heard another slight movement. "It's just a rat!" she whispered in the pitch-black aperture. I had to hurry before she moved. It was the last hour of the trial.

Only wolves defeat wolves, played the triumphant tape in my mind.

The darkest of sorcery began surging through my body. With my traitor only an inch in front of me, I could hardly contain my feelings. The scavenger began to rise . . . I was a vulture . . . losing control. *I must hurry, hurry lest she turn around.*

In total silence, I raised my spiked wing. I could feel the warmth of my beloved's body close to mine, which would soon be stone cold dead, and within seconds, without pulse. And the beating of my own pulse grew louder—faster—faster—for yes! Her time had finally come! And just before bringing down one fatal blow—very suddenly, came a rushing breeze across the chamber. Goosebumps hit the back of my neck and traveled down to my toes. I shut my eyes—a blinding flash—and everything went black.

The Gardener flashed before my vision like the sun in all its brilliance. Then a ray of light shined over me in the darkness. I was outside of my body, looking at myself from the outside, through the lens of light, which exposed my soon-to-be dark deed, holding up my spiked wing, ready to slay my betrayer.

"They are murderers from the beginning! They know nothing of love!" the Gardener's voice boomed. "Sin is lurking at your door and desires to have you. I am the Lamb, gentle and meek, but mightier than wolves." In his hands, he held a large branch that gleamed with the reddest sap in all the world. It dripped like blood down the springtime leaves. I stared, transfixed.

"Child, here I am! I am the branch. I hold out my arms and offer you love—freely—and this salve to put on your eyes—so you can see." He stared at me with his glorious, golden-brown eyes.

Without knowing all the reasons why, I reached out and grabbed onto the branch. I felt unmatchable power in it. And my heart fluttered in my chest with unspeakable warmth, like the budding of a colorful springtime that was melting all the winter out of my ice-cold heart. And with my hand, I smeared the red salve from the branch—and a soft tingle ran up my arm—I put it on my eyes—and when I opened them—I began to see.

And the Gardener was a glorious, golden god in a gleaming mist, brighter than the stars. "It is not for you to repay. I alone will wipe away every tear from your eyes, and death will not have you because the old things have passed away."

And then to my shock, all the ghosts from my past swirled in a cloud before me. Instead of haunting me, Sunbeam's own self-inflicted faults turned her face into a frown. I saw my beloved, searching for me, with a heart that was just as broken and shattered as mine. "Gilda, I'm so sorry. So very sorry!" She wept and wept into one loud rainstorm of tears. "Gilda, it was a mistake. Forgive me. I'm lost without you. Gilda, forgive me." And in Sunbeam's tears, I saw me: two as one—heartbroken—and neither one free.

Then the Gardener's voice shook the whole earth: "Let the one who wishes, take the gift of healing from my tree; let the evil person go on in his evil; let the one who does right continue to do right. The time is near. My reward is with me, to repay each person according to what they have done.

"Yes! I am coming soon!"

In a flash, I snapped out of the vision. I was back to where I began—inches from Sunbeam in the dark. And with my sharpened wing at her neck, she whispered unsurely in the pitch black, "Who's there? Gilda?"

Then very suddenly, something broke inside of me, as if I were melting from the inside out. "I . . . I *forgive* you," I whispered, so quietly she never heard me, never knowing I was ever there. And quietly, ever so quietly, I drew back my fatal wing, to spare her life. And with each breath I took, the heaviest shackles of all were breaking inside of me. And I looked away from her to face the darkness, but this time with unspeakable warmth and light, burning all the coldness away inside of me, until I finally made a complete turn—and walked away. Because for the first time in that darkness, I could see.

CHAPTER THIRTY-FIVE

GIL'DA

PRESENT
13 YEARS OLD

Holding cell, Realm of the Dark Night

I wake, shaking in a pool of sweat, gasping for air. I open my eyes to find I'm back in my cell. Coming to, I feel like I'm waking from the deepest slumber of my life. *What . . . wha . . . ?* By habit, I immediately reach for my elixir, the very last drink of it. I watch it swirl in the chalice. I . . . I no longer have a taste for it! I throw it down. The glass shatters on the floor. Excited, I grab my stone.

"Serpentine? Oh, Serpentine! You wouldn't believe what I—" And holding up my crystal, staring into the center of it, the inclusion looks like that of a lamb. *What in the name of . . . ?* And a fragrant breeze brushes my face. A pale mist whirls, and my plant is growing and filling the entire cell, which bears even more fruit, the ripest, most colorful fruit I've ever seen.

I kiss my trusty stone. "Serpentine, I see. I CAN FINALLY SEE!" And suddenly, to my shock, the inclusion of the lamb breaks the stone into two, its hardness spilling out of the center and running through the cell like a glowing, crystal stream.

Then comes the Gardner's voice like refreshing waters: "Daughter, I have come to make captivity itself a captive and to rescue prisoners from darkness. In their suffering, their minds have become depraved. They have no love in their hearts. But all have fallen short of doing the right thing. So, teach them to forgive because you have been forgiven. You can have a new mind and heart."

In the next moment, the iron walls of the cell begin to shrink and close in upon me. "The hour is up! The time has come!" I run to the cell door, collapsing to the floor, knowing freedom lies just on the other side. For my own bitter revenge had engulfed me, and my own shadow of darkness had held me prisoner.

And the door quakes as though being awakened from an ancient, fossilized sleep—and in a loud rush, it flings wide open—bright light illuminates the entire cell—and I am set free.

The Quiet Gardener embraces me on the other side. Overcome with joy, I fall down at his feet, for I know without a doubt, he is worthy of honor.

"Stand up on your feet, child." He embraces me. "You have come home."

"What about Sunbeam?" I ask. "Where is she? Will I see her again?"

"Daughter, take heart. You were held in a cell of an ethereal realm, a plane of suffering in the dark night of soul. That demon almost took your life, but by my mercy, you a entered a passage of purification, where every attachment to evil must be expelled, every blemish of the soul healed and corrected in a cleansing of love, and a chance to feel my presence so you could *see* love and know and do what is right—given a chance to enter eternity—into the vault of heaven. For I am the Lamb, the God of Justice, mightier than wolves. I descended into darkness, so you could ascend with me into light. I fill the whole universe with myself, and all the celestial realms unseen by those who refuse to open their eyes. But child, now you have seen. You will be united with your beloved again in Paradise, the City of God. Today, Sunbeam remains in the land of the living, for her time has not yet come. As for you, child, your work on this side of the chasm between life and death is not yet done.

"By my name, your beloved Sunbeam has crushed that demon from old in the land of the living, doing my work on earth. She has slayed him to dust and ash. But his spirit still roams."

The Gardener brings his glowing face close to mine. "Now, take hold of the Branch," he says. "And hold on."

I know what I must do. I am a seer. Yes, I, Gilda, transcend time and planes, into the unseen realms that are more visible than anything in the world: the world of the gods.

I stretch my arms—higher—higher—opening my wings. With the gardener's tree of life growing within me, my heart is strengthened. To my shock, I look to find my filthy black vulture wings have become new and white, gleaming like a thousand stars as I soar through the astral plane. And amazingly! My jet-black hair changes from the end of each strand, all the way up to the roots, back to its natural, golden blonde. *It's not over. Lambs defeat wolves. Oh! Lambs do defeat wolves!*

Now, the time has come to lock up the biggest wolf of all. And as I soar, I see how revenge once appeared to me as the hardest thing to do, but it wasn't at all—for a heart of stone is the hardest thing to break.

After a long stretch through the atmosphere, I swoop down from the sky to seize that ancient demon, Lord Wolford. And with my new-found sight, sharp as an eagle's eye, I descend. And going down into the abyss, I see the souls of those he deceived throughout time, from the four corners of the earth, throughout all the cities of the world.

"Please! Let us out of this place of torment!" They wail and plead with their silver cords severed in the underworld.

Wolford's minions lash back at them, "You hateful dogs! You made your choices! You gave your souls to the darkness, spewing curses and destroying lives with unforgiveness in your hearts. You have rejected love!"

And as they beg for release, I see all their silver cords, lying in thousands of piles, as many as the sand on the seashore—all severed in silver heaps around Wolford's throne of fire—the angry fire fanned by that devil who deceived them with false truth.

But now, I hold the branch. Its red blood-sap gleams down the stem. In a flash, I swoop down upon Lord Wolford.

Then all at once, he looks up at me, snarling teeth and swatting his sharp claw in fury. I swing the branch with my glorious wing, the sparkling blood splatters all over his throne. And suddenly, his throne shatters into a thousand pieces like splintered wood, adding lumber to his own sinner's fire. "Gilda! No! Gilda! Come home, Gilda! In hell you belong!" Wolford seethes and shrinks back, for he knows his time has come.

"I am Gilda, daughter of mankind. You may have scratched my heel, but I have come to crush your head!"

Then very suddenly, and with some supernatural strength, I stretch my wings and start flying at light speed, seizing the thousands upon thousands of silver cords, the heaps of broken ones from all the people he lured into darkness. And then I hold them all up with my wing like a great chain.

"Gilda! No. NOOOO!" he hisses.

"I am Gilda! You are hereby bound. You are forever chained with all of the silver cords, from all the troubled souls who sought truth, but whom you deceived and cut down in their suffering!"

In the mix of all this, I open my wings and fly with tremendous speed, circling around and around him, fast as white lightning, binding him with the great chain of silver cords. And there he will stay locked up, that liar, in the same place he bound those who rejected love, and who refused to give up their evil, their vengeance and their wicked arts—where he will be tormented day and night, for ever and ever. And before closing the shaft to the abyss on him, I shout throughout the underworld: "By this, my beloved and I have both come into the light! Sunbeam has cut you down in the flesh, and I, Gilda, in the spirit—so the two you tried to break, have slayed you—as *one*!"

Then I look up out of the abyss and into the sun, and from it the Gardener's face shines on me and urges, "Hold on to the branch!" I shut the shaft to the abyss. I quickly open my great dazzling wings, and flying out of that darkness, I shout, "To the light!"

I keep flying. UP—UP HIGHER! Until a streak like the morning dawn begins to illuminate the horizon, as if the vault of heaven opens and spreads till it shines over every flower and tree, colorful and brilliant for miles and miles. Then all at once comes the Quiet Gardener, and he is more powerful than the sun in all its radiance. He opens his arms and says:

"You have always been one of the God of Light's children, who was with you in your time of darkness, and embraces you with love, upon your return from it." Then he lifts his hand, and in it, he holds the tree of life. "Now, Gilda, after nine months in your Dark Night of Soul, you have come into the FULLNESS OF TIME."

And in the next moment, a flame flickers and rises around us, but I am not consumed by the golden fire. And to my great shock, Sunbeam materializes before me through a mystical portal, from the land of the living. She still lives on earth. She stares at me, awe-struck. And a long time goes by as she studies my face in shock. "Gilda? Oh! Gilda! Is it you?" She stares at me in astonishment then falls down, weeping. "I've been searching for so, so long. Come back, Gilda! Tell me. Tell me we will be together again!"

My heart weeps, but a good kind of weep, knowing that one day, we will be together again in the City of God. "Dear Sunbeam," I say, "I did not shrink back from death. To keep you alive, when you came to find me in Wolford's dungeon, it was too late. I fought Wolford to my death and held him back in the Valley of Dry Bones, so that you could escape. Know, Sunbeam, although separated, we both slayed him as one. Know that I still *live*. In my trouble and grief, those who are evil meant to harm me, but the God of Lights used it for my glory. I suffered greatly but have found healing and joy under his shade. Yes, I am still alive."

Then my eyes behold my own father, looking towards me in the distance of the fire. His shriveled flesh plumps out on his bones, and on his skin—the mark of the claw vanishes—and emptiness lifts from his eyes because he, too, has been freed from that devil's tricks. And in the fullness of time, which words cannot express, I understand it all. For I have forgiven my father, too. And from the land of the living, my father gazes at me with tremendous love. "Gilda, my daughter, I went back for you. I tried to save you. I was too late. We have both sorrowed deeply over the human condition and evil. But we both found truth and healing under His shade and in the true light." A tear flows down his cheek.

"I . . . I wish we could be together again," Sunbeam says, tears running down her face.

After a long moment, I encourage her. "Dear Sunbeam, you must remain in the land of the living, for your time has not yet come. We will be together again one day in Paradise. Nothing can take my love from you," I say.

"Gilda, you're free." Sunbeam says smiling. "Yes, you are finally free."

Epilogue

Since that long time ago, I wonder who else might be seeking truth. Who is out there suffering, wounded by the blades of others, locked in the prisons of their own past? And who will be the next to see? For the bars of captivity can be opened—setting all those hardened in the center like a stone into a flowing, crystal stream.

For the Quiet Gardener's words light the way, filling the whole universe: *Child, open your eyes, so you can see—and to those in darkness, hold on!*

Yes! I am coming soon!

Appendix

The existing terms below have been provided for extended knowledge.

Astral Travel (projection) – 1) a spiritual journey of the soul 2) the ability for a person's soul to transcend into other times, places, and realms 3) an out of body experience

Dark Night of the Soul – 1) derived from St. John of the Cross' poem which embodies a mystical time of refinement that eventually leads to deeper spiritual union with God 2) a spiritual journey of solitude and suffering 3) a dark, desolate time which leads to a rebirth

Familiar Spirit (or "Familiars") – 1) an evil spirit(s) serving and obeying a witch or spellcaster, usually takes the form of an animal 2) familiars (evil spirits) were popular in 16th century folklore and old magic to serve witches

Jesus – the divine Son of God in Christian theology 2) " . . . the light of the world. He who follows me will not walk in darkness but will have the light of life (*World English Bible*, John 8.12) 3) I am the way, the truth, and the life (*World English Bible*, John 14.16)

Metaphysical – 1) derived from the Greek *meta ta physika* (beyond nature) 2) beyond human perception 3) universal parts or elements of reality not easily discovered in day-to-day life 4) supernatural (*Webster's 1913*)

Tet (9) – 1) the 9th Hebrew letter which means *truth* 2) a symbol of dualism where God can make something pure from something impure 3) Tet—the idea that even when evil things happen, there is good hidden in it 4) a hidden, protective realm where things change and renew

www.ingramcontent.com/pod-prod[illegible]t-compliance
Lightning Source LLC
Chambersburg PA
CBHW030320020726
47493CB00004B/1098
* 9 7 8 1 9 5 4 [illegible] 9 6 6 6 1 *